D1080397

Yuma Breakout

Horseless and down to his last dollar, out-of-work cow-puncher Nahum Crabtree ended up in the small town of Rios. After a spell in jail, he thought his fortunes might be improving when he got taken on by a freighting outfit, especially when one of his bosses turned out to be an attractive young woman.

Yes, everything was going well – until he found himself unwittingly involved in springing a convict from Yuma Penitentiary.

And that was only the beginning of his troubles. . . .

Yuma Breakout

Jeff Sadler and B. J. Holmes

A Black Horse Western

ROBERT HALE · LONDON

ISBN 978-0-7090-8619-2

Robert Hale Limited
Clerkenwell House
Clerkenwell Green
London EC1R 0HT

www.halebooks.com

Typeset by
Derek Doyle & Associates, Shaw Heath
Printed and bound in Great Britain by
CPI Antony Rowe, Wiltshire

My husband Geoff (or Jeff as he preferred for his westerns) was working on *Yuma Breakout* before fate decreed that it was to be a project that he would never finish. Fortunately there was enough material in what he had managed to do for a completed book to be envisaged, and I thank our friend B.J. Holmes for his contribution in helping to bring it to the printed page.

Jennifer Sadler

Jeff and I go back a long way. We had many shared interests not the least being music as reflected in a chain of mutual dedications over the years on BBC's *Jazz Record Requests*. We would discuss our ongoing projects into the night and, needless to say, enjoyed each other's books. Hopefully this closeness helped me in the present task in which I have been honoured to help Jennifer develop *Yuma Breakout* into a publishable form. I can only hope we've done him justice.

B.J. Holmes

ONE

Frank Lyle tap-tapped the sidewalk with his boot. 'Now, that's what makes this place distinctive.'

At his side, Eugene Whelan dropped his head and stared blankly at the ground. 'It's just a sidewalk, boss.'

'My dear Gene, you see only a sidewalk because you've been spoiled by towns back East where, it is true, this would be nothing special. But use your eyes. Out here this ain't just any sidewalk. No wooden boardwalk like you can see in any Western town. Ain't you noticed? This is solid magnesia limestone.' His head swung as his eyes spanned the width of the walkway. 'And must be a dozen feet wide.'

He had to raise his voice against the din of a K.P. locomotive that trundled past on the track that ran plain down the middle of the main drag effectively dividing it into two separate streets. 'Ellsworth has the only such sidewalk west of Kansas City. I've heard tell of it but never see'd it.'

He waited until the train had passed, then he nodded along the street. 'And – see the stockyards there? The town boasts they're the biggest in the state.'

'Still don't get it, boss.'

Lyle sighed in mild exasperation. 'Such things are of interest to men of our calling, my friend, because they are *signs* of prosperity. And that's what we're here for – to avail ourselves of some of that prosperity.'

Lyle and his gang had been lying low, waiting for a big herd to come in to the Ellsworth railhead. Some weeks earlier, on a lone reconnaissance trip, the boss had already scouted the town and noted which was the biggest bank. Then, when he had figured a few days back that the optimum time was approaching, the six men had ridden into town. They had entered in three separate pairs and taken pallets in different lodgings posing as cowpokes on the lookout for work. The ploy of keeping apart was a precaution against arousing suspicions, but now that pens were bulging with the latest bellowing herd, the town's population had boomed accordingly with noisy, fun-seeking stockmen all over the place. Six rough riders like the Lyle gang didn't look out of place at all.

'Well,' he whispered, throwing a glance around the bustling settlement, 'looks like the plum is ready for picking.'

It was night and, as was their habit, the six had met up in the darkness some way out of town to discuss planning.

Lyle eyed the distant lights of the railhead. 'OK, men,' he said. 'I figure that by close of business tonight enough of the drovers' wages will have worked its way through the saloons and stores into the bank to make it worthwhile.'

'So we're gonna crack it tomorrow?' The question came from a large bull-necked member of the gang. His name was Hagan and there was eagerness in his voice and a glint in his black eyes.

'Yes, Bart. First thing tomorrow.'

While the others exchanged excited glances the one known as Whelen stared contemplatively at the glowing end of his cigarette. 'I can see the way your mind is working, boss, but by the same reckoning, if we leave it a few more days wouldn't we get an even *bigger* haul?'

'No, Gene. If we leave it much longer the cash will be starting to get broke up and dispersed to banks out of town. That's the way money works. It never stays in one place for long. So, get yourselves a good night's sleep, boys. We're pulling the job in the morning. And remember the drill: throughout the operation we don't address each other by our names. We ain't known in this part of the country and I aim to keep it that way. Now this is the way we're gonna handle it.'

Emily Brent stepped daintily along the wide limestone walkway, nodding politely at the few passers-by who happened to be out at such an early hour, her smile reflecting pleasure from the glow of the bright sun as it rose in the spring morning. She had the inclination to appreciate such things, as life had given her little else to think about, her nineteen years having thus far having been pleasurable and without misfortune. However, she was not to know that today that circumstance was going to change.

She proceeded sedately to the Cattlemen's Mercantile Bank and knocked on the front door.

There was a delay and then 'Yes?' came from the other side. 'Who is it?'

That she should be questioned was not abnormal but there was something in the tone that disconcerted her somewhat. She sensed a hardness in the tone. However, through the thick wooden panelling it was impossible to identify the voice and it never occurred to her that the speaker was anyone other than Mr Prendergast the manager. She ruminated on the abruptness of the manner for a second then concluded we all have our bad days, even dear Mr Prendergast.

She leant forward. 'Mr Prendergast? It is I – Miss Brent.'

A key rattled in the lock and the door creaked open just enough for her to slip within. Immediately strong hands grabbed her, a cloth was forced into her mouth and for a instant she seemed to see nothing but masked faces. Her heart pounding, she was bustled through to the manager's private office where a frantic-looking Mr Prendergast was sitting bound to his chair.

'These men are robbing the bank,' he spluttered, as though the situation needed explanation. 'They have an accomplice, Miss Brent. He's at the house with my wife.'

That particular part of the operation had been allotted to Whelan, his horse being tethered not too far from the manager's house and thus apart from those of the others which were standing in the main drag under the watchful eye of gang-member Eddie Crocker, a one-time horse wrangler.

'They say they won't hurt her or us,' the bank man

10

continued, 'just as long as we don't give them any trouble.'

While the girl was being similarly bound to a chair, Lyle gestured to the tallest member of the group to follow him to the front of the building. 'You're the best at lettering and such,' he whispered, when the two were out of earshot in the front of the building. 'Find a piece of cardboard and make a sign reading *Due to illness opening at noon*. Then fix it to the door so it can be plainly seen from outside. Pronto.'

With that he returned to the office.

'Right, Mr Prendergast,' he said, thumbing at the large safe against the wall. It was one of the new types with a combination lock. 'You tell us the numbers and nobody's gonna get hurt.'

'My mind's gone blank,' the man spluttered nervously.

Lyle patted the grip of his holstered gun. 'It's gonna be a sight blanker if you don't come up with the digits.'

Hagan's eyes glistened, black as oil, as he shot forward and swung a big fist across the seated man's chin. 'Do as the boss says, damn you!'

Lyle pulled his henchman out of the way. 'I've told you before, you meathead,' he snapped. 'No heavy stuff unless I say. Zealous ain't the word for you at times. What the hell you got for brains?'

He calmed down, took the handkerchief from the manager's top pocket and wiped the trickle of blood from the man's mouth. 'Just a matter of composing yourself and remembering, isn't it, Mr Prendergast? Get the poor man a glass of water. It might help him relax and aid his memory.'

Eventually the numbers were forthcoming. Lyle

heaved open the heavy door and appraised the stacked bills and certificates with satisfaction. 'OK, fill the saddle-bags.'

At that point the tall man, name of Wessels, returned from the front lobby. 'Sign's in place, boss.'

'Good.' He waited until the first set of bags was filled and strapped tight. 'Bring your bags and come with me,' he said, gesturing for the lanky man to follow him into a corridor that led to a side door. 'Get over to Prendergast's place. Tell Gene the job's done and to make his own way out of town. Then tell Eddie we're coming.'

Their mounts were hitched amongst a gamut of drovers' horses outside a saloon a couple of blocks down where the young Eddie Crocker was keeping his eye on them.

'Then you skedaddle,' Lyle continued. 'And remember: take things calm and easy. Look like you ain't got a care in the world. Nobody's got no reason to suspect nothin' yet.'

He opened the door to the alley and glanced both ways. 'Clear,' he said in a low voice.

As the rangy man disappeared, Lyle returned to the office. 'Now, we'll go one at a time at staggered intervals.' He waited until Shaughnessy had sealed up his bulging bags and he escorted him likewise to the side door.

'Hold it,' he whispered, pulling his head back. 'There's a couple of guys gabbing at the end of the alley.' Several minutes of furtive glances passed before he saw the men finally continue on their way. 'OK,' he said, indicating for Shaughnessy to make his exit.

Lyle looked impatiently around for Hagan, the last. What was the delay? Then he heard the sounds of cloth being torn and muffled whimpering. He dashed back into the office to see the big man crouched over the back of the woman. Taking advantage of the unexpected hold-up the man had ripped open the front of her dress and was now groaning into her hair while his hand feverishly groped her semi-exposed breast.

'You bozo,' Lyle snapped, hauling Hagan off by the scruff of his neck, 'we ain't got time for that nonsense. We gotta git!' And he pushed the man towards his loaded bags. 'Pick them up and hit the trail. And don't forget to pull your bandanna down when you get outside, you dumb cluck.'

As Hagan left, Lyle picked up the last set of bags and looked at the distraught woman as he did so. 'Real sorry about that, miss.'

He threw a final glance round the room before making his own way.

'Quiet enough back there, boss,' Wessels observed. His lanky frame was leaning against a cottonwood as he peered into the blackness of the flat terrain that they had just crossed.

'So it should be,' Lyle said. 'Nobody's on our trail yet and we been riding all day. Besides, it would have been hours before anybody found out and by then they wouldn't have a clue which way we went. We're sitting pretty.'

'When we gonna divvy up?'

'Plenty of time for that. Can't do it anyways until we got a fire to give us some light to count the money by. Meantimes you stay here on guard. I'll send up a relief after a spell.'

He made his way down the grade into the hollow which he'd decided was a good place for them to camp for the night.

'We gonna eat, boss?' Hagan wanted to know as soon as Lyle had reached the bottom. 'My guts are rumbling like billy-hell.'

'Sure we're gonna eat. You think the rest of us ain't got stomachs? Huh, drink, gorging your belly – you sure think about your gratifications.' He hadn't spoken to Hagan since the robbery. 'What is it with you, anyways? If you ain't ripping the clothes off unwilling women you're whopping guys harder than you need to. I've told you before – rein in your lusts. Just keep outa my way. You're pushing my patience.'

At the reprimand Hagan shrunk into the shadows and Lyle turned to face the remaining men. 'Gene, get the grub ready.'

As a one-time cook on a Mississippi riverboat, Eugene Whelan was a natural to be put in charge of provisions and of feeding the group.

'Meantimes, the rest of you gather kindling for a fire,' Lyle ordered. 'Down here the light won't be spotted from the trail. And Eddie, give it a quarter-hour then relieve Wessels on watch.'

It was approaching midnight. They had eaten and in the firelight Lyle was counting the money as the rest of the gang watched silently.

'Fifty thousand,' he concluded eventually. 'And some.'

'Hallelujah!' one of them exclaimed.

'I said it would be a good haul,' Lyle said. He chuck-

14

led as he studied the pile of bills. 'If only young Steve could see this – he'd know what he's missing out on. Still, he made his choice.'

'Whose Steve?' Crocker asked.

'My cousin,' Lyle said. 'We started out together on the owlhoot trail, back in the old days when we was kids. It was just small stuff then but he got cold feet, said he was gonna have a go at making it straight.'

'Where is he now?'

'Last I heard he was trying to make ends meet in someplace called Celebration. Huh, more fool him.' He counted out a couple of thousand and stuffed it into his pocket. 'Well, that's my dividend as boss.'

'Yeah, that was agreed, chief,' somebody said.

'And now for the split,' Lyle went on as he began to count out the money into six piles. 'By the way, who's on watch?'

'Whelan.'

'Fetch him down. No reason why he shouldn't get the satisfaction of seeing his cut being counted.'

He continued with building up the piles until suddenly he paused in his counting and yawned uncontrollably. 'Jeez, it's been a long day. We gotta hit the hay.'

'You ain't the only one who's looking forward to getting under a blanket,' Crocker said, his own yawning presenting him difficulty in his attempt to focus on the money being counted out by the leader. 'Don't know what the hell's got into me.'

'Don't worry,' Whelan commented with a ribbing chuckle as he joined the group. 'You're just getting old, is all.'

Lyle shook his head, opened his squeezed-up eyes and resumed his task. 'Yeah, the sooner we get some shuteye, the fresher we'll be for the long trail ahead tomorrow. We're making good time so there's no immediate worries, but we still got some hard riding to do before we're well and truly clear.'

TWO

Pat Slaughter felt the nearside wheel dig in the rut and she gripped on the reins as the shock jarred through her.

'You OK, Miss Slaughter?' Mike Tough yelled back from the lead wagon.

'Nothing I can't handle,' the young woman returned. Then she swore tightly, slack of rope coming down hard on the rumps of the mules. The animals hauled away and she breathed again, the wheel clearing to hit the bed of the trail.

The old man looked back to confirm she was rolling again and urged his own animals to resume their toil. 'Best part of the journey done now,' he shouted by way of comfort. 'Another couple of hours and we're there.'

They were delivering supplies to a mining camp up in the foothills and had been journeying since first light. The freighting company – Slaughter & Tough – had been set up years ago by Pat's father and, when he had died, she had continued the business in conjunction with her father's old partner, Mike Tough. She'd been around horses since a younker and could drive a wagon with the best. She had handled the accounting and correspondence for her father so that now she was an equal partner, that side of the concern came natural to her. The roughness of her hands attested to the fact that when it came to the physical labour of shifting stuff on and off wagons, she pulled her weight. They didn't make a fortune but it was a living.

She took off her hat, ran her fingers through her dark wavy hair, then wiped her brow as she looked ahead. The rolling sweep of brown flatland with its sparse dots of green shaded to bluish grey in the shape of the broken line of the mountains that loomed ahead.

'There'll still be daylight when we get to the camp,' Tough shouted, 'but reckon we'd best spend the night there. Ain't avoiding it.'

'Yeah, ain't avoiding it,' she mimicked. 'To boot it gives somebody a chance to muscle into a few poker games and get his hands on some of the fruit of the miners' hard-earned diggings.'

'Don't know what you're a-talking of, Miss Slaughter.'

'Ha, you're forgetting, I know you of old, Mr Tough.'

He laughed.

'Yeah,' she laughed back.

But they were tired and content from then on to continue their way in silence. And they may not have spoken for the rest of the journey had it not been for the sudden crackle of gunfire. The sharp breaking of the peace caused the woman to grab the reins like the jaws of a vice.

In the echoing chamber of the landscape it was not at once evident from whence came the sound. She looked ahead and saw her companion's right arm stabbing out as he yelled, 'There!'

Following the direction that he indicated she saw two riders fast approaching across the flat land.

The wagon drivers instinctively rapped the ribbons for increased speed but within a few seconds Tough shouted, 'We ain't gonna get clear of 'em. Only thing for it but to make a stand!'

He yanked on the driving reins to slow his mules but they veered sharply to the left and his wagon crashed over onto its side. In a cloud of dust the animals dragged it for a few more yards before giving up the task of lugging dead weight. Tough spilled to the ground, rolled and staggered to his feet. With a shake to clear his head, he dashed back to the upturned wagon, his hands scrabbling under the seat where he kept his gun.

Pat successfully brought her own wagon to a standstill. Then, to the racket of handguns and approaching hoofs, was added the crash of the woman's shotgun. No mean hand with a firearm, she had already taken cover behind her wagon and was steadily taking aim between shots.

Finally locating his own gun, Tough began to trigger the carbine.

The approaching riders fanned out to make return fire more difficult.

'You concentrate on the one coming up on your side,' Mike shouted. 'I'll try to down the other.'

Wood splintered as bullets crashed into wagon sides.

'OK!' she yelled, re-triggering her gun and staggering to the recoil.

Both riders were becoming dangerously close, but, as they neared, they were becoming bigger targets, despite their ploy of zigzagging. Pat wiped sweat from her eyes and lined up yet again. *Bang!* This time her target

19

doubled up in the saddle. The other continued his advance until he noticed his stricken comrade. He wheeled his horse around and joined the man. Continuing to shoot, he grabbed at the loosened reins. But the task of trying to get a grip became his main concern and he had to sheathe his gun. So, when he'd finally brought the animal under control his prime objective had become that of retreat and he began to lead the mount of the wounded fellow away with no more gunfire.

On the other hand, aware that the danger may not be completely over, the wagon drivers continued to send lead across the space until the failed bushwhackers were distant dots.

When he was sure the men planned no immediate return, Tough looked at the woman and emitted a 'Phew!'

Silently they continued their vigil until the attackers had completely disappeared into the Arizona heat-haze.

'Some smart shooting there, miss. Now they've tasted lead, don't think we'll see them again.' He walked round to the other side of the upturned wagon, sat with his back against the boarding and continued to stare into the distance. 'You OK, miss?'

'Yes.'

She made her way over to him. He looked exhausted. 'But more important, Mike, how are you?'

He had closed his eyes and was gripping his chest. 'Just give me a minute.'

She knelt beside him. 'You in some kind of pain, Mike?'

'It'll pass.'

'What is it? Is there something I can do?'

Her ignored her and within a few minutes he was back to normal and once more on his feet.

'What do you think the skunks were after?' she asked. 'It's not as though we're carrying bullion.'

'Who knows? Must have thought an old man and young gal were easy meat.' He looked at the spilled goods: mining tools, cooking equipment and assorted dry goods. Some of the bags were still spewing sugar and salt. Together they righted the broken containers and then he gave the wagon the once-over. 'It looks as though the thing's still trail-worthy.' He flexed his muscles looking more like his old self. 'Think you can help me right it?'

'Come on,' she said, slightly indignant that he was treating her like some frail female.

'Good,' he concluded. 'We should be able to manage it together. When we've done that, you keep vigil with those eagle eyes of yours while I salvage what I can and restack it.'

It was dark when they reached their destination but they had known they were approaching it long since – from the lights and noise of the night's carousing which was already well into its early stages. The mine and its attendant town lay deep into the foothills at the end of a box canyon, walled on three sides by sheer, looming cliffs of rock. Many tree stumps hadn't been grubbed up, and the trail wound round them, a ribbon of mud and dirt that grew into the main street. At its entrance they asked after the mercantile and threaded their way through the snarl of evening traffic. Shacks belched black smoke from

21

holes in their roofs and even at this hour steam hammers pounded deafeningly.

'Does it ever quiet down around here?' Mike asked, when they'd located the mercantile and its manager.

'Ain't no such thing as day or night once you get into the mines,' the man said. 'There's always something going on: revelry and men working shifts around the clock.'

As they started unloading, Mike explained about the attack upon them.

'Better tell the constable,' the manager said.

'You got law here?'

'Kind of. Not sanctioned by the territorial authorities, you understand. Just a guy employed to keep the peace. Joe Shields, paid for by a levy on the miners. We call him constable. He likes that. Even got one of the metalworkers to hack out a badge for his chest. He's a good man. Was a miner himself in the days when he could wield a pick so he knows the ins and outs of the business.' He waved along the space that served as the main drag. 'You'll find him yonder.'

When unloading was complete they watered the mules. Then they left the wagons alongside the mercantile and found the shack with 'Constable' scrawled crudely on the door.

Constable Shields was burly and thickset, with a battered rawhide face that looked like the man had used it alone to chip ore out of the rock.

'Couple of *hombres* tried to drygulch us on the way in,' Mike informed him after explaining who they were.

'What happened?'

The old man recounted the episode. 'Young Pat here

22

winged one of the jaspers,' he said in conclusion. 'Don't know how bad but that's why they made off.'

Shields eyed his female visitor. 'Good on yuh, missy.' Then he asked for descriptions of their attackers.

'The chowderheads were too far distant for anything precise,' Mike said. 'Pat had put her slug in one before they got close enough for us to make out details. Just a couple of guys. You any ideas?'

The constable shook his head. 'Ain't nobody I could name. And nobody's come in here wounded as far as I know. Attacking from a distance like that with side-arms tells me they were greenhorns at the game. Figure they wus just opportunists – and probably young at that. Damn varmints. A place like this attracts all kind of human dross.'

He proudly thumbed his badge. 'That's why they got me. I try to keep tabs on who's who but there's so much coming and going around here it ain't a precise business. As to your unfortunate incident, could be anybody after a dollar. See, most consignments leaving the camp are valuable – either money or ore – so we're prepared for any shenanigans and have armed guards on all traffic out of the place. The few crooks that tried anything when our tent city was getting established ended up with a touch of lead poisoning. News got around that outward consignments were well guarded so this trouble you had suggests that some remaining scum have turned their attention to incoming traffic. They'll know that takings won't be as good but anything is better than nothing for varmints who ain't got a legitimate trade in their limbs.'

The sound of what could be some kind of ruckus broke the quiet of the room and the constable cast an ear. 'Seems like my services might be called for. Time for the first of my evening rounds, anyways. So if you'll excuse me, folks.' He took his gunbelt from a peg on the wall and settled it around his waist. 'Leastways, you got through the escapade unscathed. That's the main thing.'

He fixed the buckle, then guided them toward the door. 'One last thing, I suggest you give thought to taking on some kind of guard yourselves. Especially if you're aiming to come out this way again. Might not be so lucky next time.'

Outside they watched him make his way along the crowded makeshift boardwalk. 'Despite your fancy shooting, missy,' the old man said to his companion, 'I think he's right about us getting someone to ride shotgun.'

THREE

Nahum Crabtree was trudging wearily along the trail when he heard metal rims on grit behind him. He turned to see a stagecoach lurching into view over the ridge that he himself had traversed some time past.

He dropped his burdens on the dusty verge, slumped beside them and waited. As the vehicle approached he hauled his tall frame to the vertical and waved.

'Lost my hoss to a rattler a-ways back,' he shouted to the driver as the stage crunched to a dusty standstill beside him. 'Get a lift to the nearest town?'

'Sure thing, pilgrim,' the man said, patting the seat beside him. 'Hop aboard. We go as far as Rios.'

'Sounds fine to me.'

Nahum heaved his saddle and saddle-bags onto the rack, then pulled himself alongside the driver.

'Had to shoot my hoss,' he said, as the stage pulled away. 'Had him under me a few years. Real sad to see him go.'

He reflected on the memory for a moment. 'By the time I'd put him away the damn rattler had found hisself a rock for cover but I poked him out with a stick and shot the critter's head off. But it didn't ease matters much.

I'm gonna miss that hoss.'

'Don't recognize you. What brings you out this way?'

'Got laid off as a trail-drover. Beef business's took a downturn. You might have heard how bad things are getting out on the range. So, looking for work is head of my list at the moment.'

'Don't know if Rios is your best bet, pilgrim. Ain't nothing but a hick town. A kid with no hairs on his chin could spit from one end of the main drag to the other.'

He stepped down from the stage, throwing a 'Thanks' to the driver. The gratitude he showed was not only for the ride but the waiving of any travel fee.

The town of Rios consisted of shacks lined up on either side of the trail. There was a narrow, dusty unpaved main street and maybe one of each establishment that a town required. He located a drovers' dosshouse, passed over a few coins to reserve a bed and dumped his gear.

Back outside he strolled along the drag. He made out fading letters scrawled above a doorway proclaiming THE HOUND DOG SALOON. He spanked dust from his clothing and headed in.

Inside, he bellied up to the pine bar, the brass foot-rail bracing under his boot. As the barman was otherwise occupied in collecting glasses, Nahum took the opportunity to scour his pockets and laid down the resulting handful of bills and small heap of coins on the bar. He eyed them and made a tally of his resources. He had no job, no horse and maybe enough dollars to see him through to the end of the week. When he'd done his totalling he looked around the wretched room, reflective of a wretched town, he reckoned. Seems the stage-driver had probably been right about the low odds on getting any work in the place.

As the barman came back to the bar, the visitor returned the bulk of his monetary assets to his pocket leaving a couple of coins before him and ordered a beer.

He glanced around the room, noting the place held only a handful of drinkers besides himself. Further along the unplaned pine a couple of strong-smelling men in overalls were making their way down their glasses. Across the room a foursome was playing cards. An elderly fellow, his fiery-coloured nose strongly suggesting he was a regular, was slumped in a log seat close to the door, dazedly studying what was sure-fire not his first empty glass of the day.

Nahum took a reflective draught of his own drink. Wasn't the best he had ever tasted but at least it shifted some dust and was cold, pleasantly cooling his throat as it made its way down.

Some minutes later he was getting to the bottom of the glass when one of the card-players withdrew and headed for the door.

Nahum paid him little mind until a minute or so on, a voice came from the table: 'Fancy making up a hand, stranger?'

He had long learned it was not advisable to play cards with locals in an unfamiliar town. On the other hand, for a few cents it was a way of getting to know, and get known by, locals; factors that could be useful when asking about work. So he broke his rule.

'What's the game?'

'Blackjack.'

27

'Why not?' he said, and moved over to the table.

After a couple of hands one of the men opposite him drained his glass. 'Hold the play there, fellers, while I restock my glass.'

He staggered over to the bar. 'Another one, Jed.'

'You've had enough, Andy,' the barman said. 'You been sinking the stuff all morning.'

'I'll say when I've had enough.'

The barman sighed wearily. 'I really think you should mosey home and get your head down.'

'I will – when I see fit. Now are you gonna serve me or not, mister?'

'OK, *Mister* Andy Booker, one more and that's it.'

'OK,' the man repeated with the self-satisfied confidence of one who sees himself as having gotten the better of an exchange.

He lurched back to the table with his refilled glass. 'Right, deal 'em.'

'I don't think you're in a state to play anymore, Andy,' one of the men said, gathering the cards into a neat stack and placing them to one side.

'Not *you* as well,' Booker growled.

'On your head be it,' the man responded. 'But another five minutes then I'm off.'

Play resumed. Nahum won a hand but lost several in a row. Then it came to his deal and he hit a winning streak.

'Funny how you've started winning once you got the deck in your hand,' the drunken man slurred.

'Run of the cards,' Nahum said, dealing again.

When the puncher won that one too, Booker snarled, wiping a mixture of beer and drool from his mouth with the back of his hand. 'I figure you as a hustler, stranger.

28

You been dealing off the bottom of the deck.'

Fast regretting the breaking of his rule, Nahum saw no advantage in arguing with the man in his inebriated state and pushed the cards to one side. 'Your friends are right. We shouldn't play anymore. I'll just say thanks and make my way.'

'You ain't making your way no place,' Booker said, and he rose, his fingers dancing above the handle of his sidearm. The other two players scattered from the table.

'Draw,' Booker grunted.

'I ain't drawing on nobody,' Nahum said. 'And I ain't no cheat. Chris'sake, we been playing for cents here. That worries you, have your money back. I've had a toilsome day and ain't looking for no bother.' And he pushed the small pile of coins away.

'You ain't getting off that easy,' Booker persisted. 'I said draw.'

'That's enough,' the barman boomed, a 12-gauge Greener suddenly appearing in his hands from beneath the bar. 'You know the rules. Settle your differences outside.'

Nahum looked at the heavy gun and back at Booker. 'OK, let's talk about this outside. And I mean *talk*.'

Outside the sun blasted the dirt street with its potholes and wagon-ruts as the two men faced each other a few steps from the saloon.

'This is crazy,' Nahum said.

'Go for your gun, you bunko-steer,' the other said, stepping back and working his fingers.

Nahum sighed and lowered his head so that all his opponent could see was his hat brim. 'OK, if you ain't gonna change your mind – what do you do for a living?'

29

'What the hell's that got do with anything?'

'Listen, it's you persisting with seeing this thing through so just humour me for a second.'

'If it's any business of yours, when I'm on a payroll I lay my hands to carpentering.'

The hat didn't move. 'OK, either walk away or make your play.'

'Cut the squawking. Get on with it.'

The puncher's hat brim rose so the two men were again eye to eye. 'If that's the way it's gonna be, ready when you are.'

There was a long delay. The carpenter stood, nonplussed by the exchange. What has my job got to do with things? he asked himself. He grunted, dismissed the query and his gun came out.

There were three explosions. Two loud, one kind of squelchy. The first was the sound of Nahum's gun; the second was his opponent's boot bursting in a bloody mess; the third was the man's gun firing harmlessly into the dirt before he dropped to the ground groaning.

Nahum stepped forward and picked up the man's fallen gun while sheathing his own. 'Sorry about that, pal. Hope the damage ain't too much. Maybe some skin off your toe at worst.' He turned to the crowd on the boardwalk. 'Somebody get this feller over to the doc and keep his gun in a safe place for a spell.'

'I'll take *that* gun – and *yours*.'

The booming voice came from the opposite side of the street. Nahum turned to see a man packing a star and a levelled gun.

Each of the items exerted its own form of authority. Nahum considered the figure and its symbols for a second then said, 'He forced me into it, Sheriff,' as he complied with the lawman's request.

The officer pointed further down the street. 'Just keep a button on that lip of yours and head for the law office yonder.'

Once inside the building, the sheriff ordered the cowman to remove his gunbelt and herded him into a cell at the rear of the building. He locked the barred door, then requested the prisoner's name and circumstances.

'OK, Mr Nahum Crabtree, what's your side of the events?'

'The guy made the play, Sheriff,' Nahum said when he had given his account. 'Like I said outside, he forced me into it. I tried my best to cool him down but he was a tad the worse for drink.'

'That's just what you say, stranger. Fact is, I don't like gunplay in my town.' Then his voice softened a mite as he added, 'On the other hand I don't cotton to jailing an innocent man, so you're gonna stay here until I've got to the bottom of things.'

'Wow,' Mike Tough said to Pat Slaughter as they stood outside the dry goods store. 'That's the kinda guy we could use riding shotgun on our wagons.'

They'd been loading up with coffee and flour when they'd witnessed the confrontation a little further down the street.

'Yeah,' the girl affirmed, 'he sure can handle himself. Pity he's a no-good gunslinger. Figure we'd be taking on more than we bargained for with a feller like that.'

She had no more interest in the matter and looked

along the street in the other direction. 'While we're in town let's call in at the smithy's and check if he's rerimmed that wheel. He's had it long enough.'

It was some twenty minutes later that the lawman returned to his office. He came straight to the cell and unlocked it with a flourish. 'You're free to go, mister.'

Nahum rose from the pallet on which he'd been resting. 'That's welcome news.'

'Yeah. I've heard enough witnesses testifying to your side of the story to know the rights and wrongs of the situation.'

He ushered his ex-prisoner into the front office and handed him his gunbelt.

'Obliged that you should be so prompt in giving a stranger a fair deal,' Nahum said, as he settled the rig around his hips.

'Must admit,' the sheriff said, 'Andy Brooker has been known to be a liability when he's downed some sauce but this is the first time the bozo's pushed things so far.'

'Well, thanks again.'

The sheriff put out his hand. 'Jim Gallatin; pleased to make your acquaintance. Sorry about the inconvenience, Mr Crabtree.'

Nahum forced a smile in response. 'Likewise. I know you wus only doing your job.'

'Unfortunate that your first coming to town was made so unwelcoming. Rios is a little town. Quiet, don't often get gunplay and stuff.'

'As we're getting sociable now, any idea where a guy can find gainful employment hereabouts?'

'As I said, it's a small, quiet place. The way things are

at the moment, only prosperity in the whole region is up at the diggings in the foothills.'

'The foothills you say. Maybe I'll give the mines a try afore I ride on.'

The lawman thought on the matter. 'I wouldn't advise it.'

'Why not?'

'For a start, I reckon that'd be a hit-and-miss affair for a newcomer. Jobs are pretty sewed up out there by now. But more importantly, if I were you I'd leave the locality itself before someone aims to redress a grievance.'

'Andy Booker?'

'Andy Booker.'

Nahum touched his hat as he made for the door. 'Thanks for the advice.'

'Before you go,' the lawman said, 'folks tell me you asked what Andy's trade was. Why did you do that?'

'As the guy was plain determined to push the confrontation I needed to make a decision – what would incapacitate him the least, so it was a matter of hand or foot. The way I saw it, to make a living as a carpenter like he said, he needed two hands and I guessed maybe a gammy foot wouldn't hamper him too much in that line. So that's what I went for.'

The lawman whistled. 'You can be that accurate?'

'Sometimes you have to be.'

'You ain't some kind of gunhawk, are you?'

Nahum chuckled. 'No. Just a cattle drover who's been at the game long enough to be able to handle the tools of his trade – horses, ropes, guns and a whole mess of necessary paraphernalia.'

FOUR

'Hey, that guy we saw in the shoot-out, he's no yahoo gunhawk,' Mike Tough said as he entered the kitchen. 'I just dropped in at the Hound Dog for a quick drink before coming back, you know, just to see what's what.'

Pat Slaughter looked up from her pastry-making. 'Yeah, just to see what's what,' she said with a wry smile and waggle of her head. 'I know, you just *dropped* in.'

'Anyways, Sheriff let him out of jail. Scuttlebutt around the bar is that he's an out-of-work drover who's come to town looking for a job. The lead-throwing was all Andy Booker's doing. You know Andy, he's caused trouble before with drink. Had too much as usual and for some pie-eyed reason pushed the guy into gunplay.'

'Why are you telling me?'

'I think he's worth a try, Pat. We said we needed somebody. We know he can handle himself gunwise. Jeepers, we saw that out on the street.' The oldster mimed a fast draw. 'And if he's a seasoned steer-handler he knows animals and should be able to cut it with mules and wagons.'

'Mike, we don't know anything about him apart from

34

the fact he's a fast draw. All this stuff about him being an ordinary guy, some out-of-work drover, is the talk of your rumpot friends.'

'Oh yeah, I agree it's a matter of finding out if he's trustworthy. But we could do that by taking him on for a probationary period.'

'I don't know, Mike. I'm particular about who I have in the house.'

'We don't have to let him in the house. He's bedding down at the drovers'. He'd just be an employee who comes in the morning and leaves at the end of a day's shift. And who else do we know who would fit the bill?'

She didn't say anything, so he continued, his voice now taking on a definite negative tone. 'Even so it ain't a sure thing he'd want the job.' He knew she liked a challenge and this approach was another ploy. 'If we offered it him, he might not take it. No guarantee.'

She thought about it. 'How much does a cowpoke earn these days?'

'Dunno exactly. But not much, so reckon we could pay him more than he's used to. That should make it attractive.'

'I was thinking how *low* an offer to make him.'

The man chuckled. 'Forever the businesswoman. That's som'at you get from your pa.'

Mike found Nahum a block along from the Hound Dog. The cowpoke had gone in the saloon in hopes of making his peace. The customers had cold-shouldered him but the barman was an understanding fellow. So Nahum had bought a drink, asked the barman if he knew of work. The man didn't and had suggested that if the stranger

35

aimed to stay in the town, for the sake of harmony he shouldn't patronize his establishment for a spell.

So it was that Nahum had dropped his rear into a seat a little further down the street. He'd been watching the town go about its business when Mike presented himself and made the offer of riding shotgun for the freighters.

'I know steers and horses but don't know much about mules,' Nahum explained. To him the critters ranked not much above skunks and coyotes in the grand scheme of things.

'They're much the same – only a sight more cussed.'

The cowman rubbed the dark stubble of his chin. Another issue was he didn't cotton to the notion of his gun being the centre of his employment. Then, 'What the hell, I'm down to my last cents. I'll try my hand at anything.'

Days passed. He quickly got the hang of things: loading, unloading and hauling freight around the locality. Even developed a modicum of respect if not affection for the mules. More important, he took to the owners of the outfit and they took to him; so much so that the relationship of employer-employee soon mellowed to one of friendship.

One noontime the two men returned from delivering building materials to a construction site and took their lunch as usual in the main house. When they'd finished a filling plate of steak and vegetables Mike took a smoke while Nahum helped Pat with the dishes as was becoming his habit. Not only was it his nature to want to make a contribution to such chores, but under torture he might have admitted to some attraction toward the

36

female half of the outfit.

'Hey, Nahum,' Mike shouted after a while. 'Come and look at this.'

Nahum put down the wiping cloth. 'Excuse me, Pat.'

'Look at this,' the other said, pointing to the paper he had been reading when Nahum came back into the dining area. 'Fame, kiddo! You've made the front page of the local rag.'

Nahum cast a quick eye over it. 'Huh,' he grunted. 'Makes me out as some kind of gun wizard. Don't cotton to that notion at all.'

'Ah, but there's an upside,' Mike said. 'Everything's got an upside if you look for it. If you bothered to read the small print, you'd have noted that the editor got Andy Booker to say a few words for the record. Andy ain't a bad guy really and when the bozo was sober he admitted to the paper that the incident was all his fault. The printed statement's worth taking a note of, my young buckaroo. If you should think of staying with us a while, his comment taking full blame for the ruckus should help you get along with the townsfolk.'

'Like they say, everything's got its upside,' the young man said, with an ironic stress.

As he moved towards the door in order to resume his kitchen chore, Nahum glanced at a piece of paper tacked to the wall. 'And don't fall asleep over your coffee, Mr Tough,' he said in a mock authoritarian tone. 'According to the schedule we got a heap of furniture to deliver to some homestead out in the sticks this afternoon.'

Pat chuckled as she handed him a cloth. 'A sure sign you're settling in – you're getting to know our Mr Tough.'

Days became weeks. Nahum fell more easily into the rhythm of daily toil: riding, tending to the mules, maintaining the wagons. Amongst his trips out, he rode shotgun on several trips to the mining camp with Mike and they never had a hint of any more trouble.

From the beginning Nahum had shared their table and had showed himself to be polite and companionable. One Saturday night he stayed later than usual after supper and the threesome had a convivial evening singing to the accompaniment of Mike's accordion.

'What about letting him stay permanent at the house?' Mike asked Pat, when their visitor had finally bidden them goodnight. 'He's been with us some time now and I reckon he's proved himself a regular guy. Besides, it must be rough in that smelly drovers' shack where he lays his head.'

'I don't know, Mike. It's a big step, taking someone into your house.'

'Can't do no harm, gal. He ain't put a foot wrong here or on the job. I tell you, you really get to know a feller working beside him day to day and he's OK. And it'd be better all round. What do you say?'

'Maybe,' the girl said. She did some last minute tidying up in preparation for retiring then said, 'Yeah, why not. He can have Pa's old room. It's lying empty and him staying there won't cost any.' She thought about it, then winked in an exaggerated fashion. 'Besides, it'll give me a chance to get hold of those rancid clothes of his and give them a good soaking in the tub. Like someone says, everything's got its upside.'

*

A month had passed uneventfully when Pat looked out of the kitchen window to see Mike approaching with an uncharacteristically crestfallen look to his old features.

'You OK?' she asked as he came through the door. 'You don't seem your usual chipper self.'

He seemed oblivious to her query and returned a question of his own. 'Where's Nahum?'

'Fixing a wheel on the Studebaker, why?' She continued studying him. 'What's the matter, Mike? You're looking a mite down in the mouth.'

For a moment it seemed like his mind was elsewhere but eventually her words filtered through and his face brightened. 'Oh, am I? Sorry about that, missy. Down? I don't see why. I'm bringing some good news. I got us a contract.'

'You have?' Then she put feigned reprimand into her voice, 'Makes a change from you leaving it to me to drum up business all the time.'

'Be fair, gal. You know I leave it to you deliberately. A lotta guys can't resist a pretty face. With a lot of bozos, their business-sense goes plumb out of the window the moment you walk in.' His mood seemingly forgotten, he continued the exchange in a bantering mode and wagged a finger. 'And don't tell me you don't know it and use it. You get the contracts and a good margin to boot. But I've proved I can do it too – without waggling my hips or fluttering my eyelids.'

'What's this deal then?'

'Taking lumber out to Yuma.'

'Yuma? That's a long stretch for our outfit. How did you get it?'

He winked. 'Like the old saying: it ain't what you know but who you know.'

'And who's supplying the lumber?'

'Cahill's wood shop here in town.'

'Somebody *has* pulled some strings.'

'Yeah.' He rubbed his hands again. 'Upshot is, the authorities are aiming to do some building out at the penitentiary and we got the freighting end of the contract. And what's more – it's big bucks *and* payment up front.'

He pulled some bills out of his pocket and dropped them on the table. 'Stick them in the kitty, missy.'

Pat gasped as she counted them. 'Two hundred bucks! Jehosphat, somebody did pull strings. This definitely makes a change from trading in chickens.'

At that point Nahum came through the door. 'I remounted the wheel, Pat. Like new.'

'Good,' the woman said. 'By the way Mike's fixed a deal.'

She looked at her partner to give confirmation but he seemed to be back in his trance.

'Mike,' she prompted.

'Oh, yeah,' he said. 'A deal. Delivery two days from now. Long haul – a consignment of timber to Yuma.'

'Yuma? I ain't a native boy but from what I'm learning of local geography that sure is some long haul.'

'On that point, pal, you ain't wrong.'

The following day, late afternoon, the two men took the wagon to Cahill's woodshop to collect the load.

As they entered the yard, Nahum was aware of the comforting smell of wood shavings. Reminded him of his old man's woodshed when he was a kid. They were directed to an open door and reversed the wagon through it for ease of loading.

'Hey, Crabtree!'

Nahum glanced in the direction of the voice. A fellow was limping towards him. It was the guy with whom he'd had the confrontation on his first day in Rios. What was the fellow's name? Andy Brooker, that was it.

Apprehensive of his reception, he turned more completely to face the approaching man.

'How you doing, pal?' the man said.

'OK,' Nahum returned. 'But more crucially, how are you doing?'

The man grunted amiably. 'Little bit of skin missing off the side of my little toe. Saw the doc again last week, says another couple of months and I won't miss it all.'

'Glad to hear it, mister. I'm sorry it had to come to that but you didn't give me much leeway back there, you know.'

'Hell, it's me who should be apologizing to you, acting like a damn fool the way I did. From what I gather, seems that you sought to do the minimum damage to stop me. I'm sure obliged for that. Reckon there's a lotta guys would have put my lights out permanent – and they would have been justified. Anyways, turns out you did me another favour, too.'

'Another favour? How come?'

'They did a piece about the incident in the local paper.'

'Yeah, I saw it,' Nahum said shaking his head. 'Made me out as some kind of pistolero rather than the ordinary cowpoke that I am.'

Brooker nodded in the direction of his boss. 'I worked for Mr Cahill a-ways back but he dumped me 'cos of my drinking. Anyways, he saw the item in the rag too. Took pity on me and offered me my old job back provided I kept off the booze – and here I am!'

Nahum raised his eyebrows in response to the information, 'So, all's well that ends well.'

'Yeah. Anyways, what are you doing here in our little woodshop?'

'I'd come to town looking for work. Happen that Slaughter and Tough, the freight people, gave me a job. They got a contract to deliver lumber. We're here to collect it.'

The man nodded. 'Ah, that consignment. I been working on it.'

Back at base Mike got out a map to plan the next day's journey.

'It's only one wagonload,' he said, as Pat looked over his shoulder, 'but it's such a long journey it needs two of us. So that's me and Nahum, OK with you?'

She looked askance. It hadn't occurred to her it should be otherwise. 'Why ask me? You're getting along so well together, it's a natural for the two of you.'

FIVE

'So this is Yuma,' Nahum said as they pulled in alongside the river. The journey to reach the confluence of the Gila and Colorado had taken them the best part of a day, and had been achieved without incident. They rested for a while and took in the scene, watching the endless stream of goods from the West Coast being loaded onto steamboats for shipment upriver. He looked across the waterway to Fort Yuma, the original basis for the town, perched on a hill on the western bank.

'We've made it early,' the old man said. 'Ain't due to deliver till tonight.'

Nahum grunted in a way that displayed some lack of understanding. 'What's wrong with delivering now? Then we can start back before it gets dark and bed down under the stars.'

Mike screwed up his face. 'Stars? Hell, I'm an indoor man.' An authoritativeness suddenly entered his voice. 'Besides, we gotta follow the schedule. The deal says deliver at sundown and that's what we do.' He brightened again. 'Anyways, it'll give us the opportunity to grab a bite to eat.'

Nahum shrugged off his bewilderment at his companion's fluctuating tone and they rode into town passing adobes, buildings of wattle-and-daub and ramshackle fences made of octotillo ribs.

Eventually they came to a mud block labelling itself as a cantina. It didn't look much but to two hungry men it gave off an appetizing aroma.

'We'll eat here,' Mike said. 'We can watch the wagon from the window. This close to a prison you don't know what kind of folk are floating about. Last thing we want is someone riding off with the goods.'

After they'd finished off a filling meal of *frijoles* and *tortillas*, Mike lit a smoke and contemplated his companion across the table. 'Listen,' he said in a low tone after he'd double-checked no one was in listening distance. 'It's time to tell you something. I guess it might sound kinda rum, but for the purposes of this piece of business we're operating under a different name.' He took out a piece of paper. 'Memorize that. It's the name of the enterprise.'

Nahum looked at the sheet. It was an official-looking bill with the legend 'Sughrie and Company. Gadsen' printed elegantly at the top.

'Had it printed specially,' the old man said. 'That's me, Bill Sughrie. And we operate out of Gadsen.'

'We do? Where's that?'

'Little place to the south of here. Now, what do you want to call yourself?'

'Whoa, whoa, whoa,' Nahum said, raising his hand. 'What the hell's this all about, Mike? Don't think I ain't noticed you being up and down all the time.'

'Hey,' his companion came back in a low but firm

voice, 'I've just told you, I'm *Bill*, not Mike. Bill Sughrie, got it?'

Nahum huffed in frustration. 'I don't like this – *Bill*. Entering a prison under false names. Something smells.'

'Don't worry your drover's head about it. It's just a convenience for commercial reasons. Competing tenders and such. Being a cattleman you might not understand these things.'

'Bullshit, Mike, Bill, whoever you are.'

The oldster looked about. 'Keep your voice down.'

'Listen, we'd better get something straight. I ain't saying I'm a goody-goody, far from it. I done my share of carousing, especially in my younger days. And I helped bust up saloons after many a long drive. I've used my fists and pulled a gun when I had to. But I ain't never gone out of my way to break the law in my life. That's the way I was brung up and that's the way I am.'

'Hold your hosses, young 'un,' Mike hissed, eyes flitting from side to side in fear of being overheard. 'Fact is, coming all this way with a heavy load needed two on the wagon and I couldn't involve Pat.'

'Couldn't involve Pat, eh? I see – but you could involve *me*. Well, I *ain't* involved.'

'Hey, my young friend, why do you think I stuffed a big bill in your shirt pocket before we started out?'

Nahum's mouth pulled a look that registered incomprehension.

'That means,' Mike said, 'you're already involved.'

'Oh, no, I'm not. Not in something criminal.'

'Take my word for it: it ain't criminal. Like I told you, we're using assumed names for business purposes.'

Nahum took the bill from his pocket and studied it.

'OK, I'll see it through but you and I are gonna have a serious talk about things when we get back.'

'That's better,' Mike said, his voice softening. 'So, what about your name? You need something different.'

Nahum shook his head indifferently. 'No idea.'

Mike grinned. 'You look like a Frank to me. That's it: Frank Anderson. Remember that just in case.'

Just as the sun was setting they rolled up to the Sallyport, the entrance to Arizona's infamous prison. Mike showed his paper and they were allowed through. Once past the gate Nahum was struck by the smell, one of cloying unhealthiness. Drains, maybe even sewage. Here and there a shuffling convict in chains.

A guard directed the visitors to the wood-shop. They rolled between buildings eventually reaching a yard.

'The cons will help me unload,' Mike said, as he drew back the tarp on the wagon after they had pulled in. 'Go and share a smoke with a guard for a while, something like that.'

'Hell, why?'

'What you don't see you don't know, *Frank*.'

Nahum looked around the yard. 'Ain't nothing I can do about this now, is there?'

'Nope. And remember, if it comes up, you're Frank Anderson working for the Sughrie outfit out of Gadsen.'

The younger man shrugged in token compliance and meandered across the open space.

He nodded to a sentry leaning against an adobe wall and they exchanged a few inconsequential words while he took a smoke. But his mind was on the bizarre circumstances, pondering why subterfuge should be necessary

46

for a simple delivery of timber. As he glanced casually across the dark yard he wondered if he might be unwittingly involved in something that could get him in chains and dressed in sackcloth in a stinking rat-hole like this. Why the need for false names when dropping off a simple load of wood, for Chris'sake? He just didn't get it.

A quarter-hour later the two men were back in the wagon and set to leave. They trundled once more along the dark avenues, then through the gate and into the night air.

Nahum was glad when he heard the gate clang shut behind him and breathed deeply, aware that the stuff he pulled into his lungs was clean and represented freedom.

'See,' Mike whispered when they were well clear. 'Told you there'd be nothing to it – and nothing to worry about.'

'Huh – and suppose I can call you Mike again?'

'Yeah.'

Still bemused, his companion had no other comment other than, 'Anything you say, boss.'

SIX

'Hell, I need a piss.'

The voice was a growl and came from behind, scaring the daylights out of Nahum if not so much his companion.

It was now pitch black and they had just mysteriously turned off the main trail. Nahum had questioned the change of direction but had been told they were just completing the business.

Surprise in his eyes, Nahum whirled round at the sound of the grunted articulation to his rear. 'What the—?'

In the gloom he could make out a tottery figure emerging from under the tarp.

'Rocking of the wagon put me to goddamn sleep,' the man said. 'Lost track of time, everything. Where the hell are we?'

'Figure the rendezvous ain't too far,' Mike said.

'Huh.' The man grunted in a tone that said nothing about his demeanour. 'At least now we're off the trail, there's no chance of anybody seeing us.' Then he vaulted over the wagon side.

Mike stayed the mules and the two men watched their erstwhile passenger relieve himself in the gloom.

'Who in tarnation's that?' Nahum whispered to his companion, as they listened to the voluminous cascade.

'Don't you two need to stretch your legs?' the man said with his back to them, before the old man could respond to Nahum's question.

On the suggestion the two worked their way along the seat.

'Ain't you gonna answer me?' Nahum said to his companion, as they dropped to the ground. Although nothing was still forthcoming from his partner, things began to click and he nodded his head. 'Bits and pieces are starting to make sense. I might be a bottom-of-the-heap brush-popper but I ain't all that dense. We've sprung that guy from jail, ain't we? *That*'s what all the subterfuge was about.'

Catching the comment, the ex-con laughed and he turned from his completed task, jerking a thumb towards Nahum. 'Huh, whoever this guy is, he catches on quick, don't he?'

He moved back towards them and eyed Mike. 'Well, if he's the greenhorn around here, I figure you're the boss of this wagon outfit, eh, old-timer? So give me some names – not that I need 'em.'

'I'm Bill Sughrie and this here's' – Mike faltered as he fought to recall Nahum's alias – 'Frank. Frank Anderson.'

'You don't seem too sure, Bill,' the man said.

'Like I said, Frank's a new boy. Ain't been with the outfit long.'

The man nodded. 'OK, Bill and Frank, you done a

good job here.'

Mike turned and began to walk the rising track ahead, quickly to be swallowed up by the shadows.

'Hey, where are you going?' the passenger shouted into the darkness.

'I need to check on bearings,' came a disembodied voice.

The man cursed and went over to the wagon. 'So, young 'un, you've been helping me out of the can and didn't know it, eh?' he chuckled as he walked round the vehicle giving it a close inspection. 'How come?'

'I work for the freighting company and just thought this caper was a run-of-the-mill job. Only difference was, it was a mite further out than usual, is all.'

The man poked around, came back from his circuit of the wagon and leant against the side. He looked into the blackness and didn't seem happy about something. Was his irritation due to his not being able to see Mike? Nahum wondered. Then the man's manner lightened. 'You got a smoke, pal?'

'Sure.' Nahum handed over the makings. 'Help yourself.'

The cigarette was quickly and adroitly assembled. The man handed back the makings and lit up. In the flare of the match Nahum had his first chance to get a clear picture of the ex-convict's face. The main thing that registered before the flame died was a white gash through the man's right eyebrow. Like a bad knife slash he'd suffered sometime.

'You know Tyler?' the man wanted to know.

'Tyler? Nope, don't know the feller. Means nothing to me.'

The other chuckled. 'Jeez, you don't know much at all, do you?'

Nahum let the comment ride as Mike's footsteps sounded again.

'What were you looking for?' the man asked, as the oldster emerged from the murk.

'They said to look out for a light to the north-west. It's faint but I eventually spotted it. Maybe not much than a mile. Difficult to tell in the dark. Could be a mile; reckon two miles at the most.'

'Two miles, eh?' the man said. 'That's near enough.' He turned and, before either of the other two was aware of what was happening, he had whipped the rifle from under the seat where they normally kept it and was levelling it their way. Nahum then realized how the fellow had carefully inspected the vehicle while Mike was absent. It was now clear that he had been doing so in order to locate a gun.

'Shuck your side-arms,' the man snapped, noisily levering the weapon.

'No need for this, Mr Whelan,' Mike said. 'Hey, we're on your side, remember? It was us got you out of the slammer for Chris'sake.'

'I'm just being careful, Bill. Now do as I say.'

After they had dropped their weapons the man collected them and appraised the two figures before him. Then said, 'Reckon your closest to my size, Anderson. Get your duds off.'

'The hell I will,' Nahum snarled.

The rifle jabbed towards him.

'Better do as he says, Frank,' the oldster advised.

'Frigging mess this is – *Bill*,' Nahum said, as he began

51

to empty his pockets in preparation to parting with his clothing.

'Leave the stuff in the pockets,' Whelan snapped. 'Especially the money. I'll need that.'

'My dough?'

'You bet, brush-popper,' the man said, jabbing the rifle forward again. 'Leave everything in the pockets.' He watched Nahum as he disrobed. 'Just your top gear,' he chuckled. 'You can hang on to your underwear and dignity.'

'Thanks for nothing.'

Taking the clothes, the man kept his distance from the other two while he dressed himself, the exercise conducted slowly as he kept himself close to a cocked pistol he had carefully laid butt-first on the wagon seat.

'Now whatever cash you got, old-timer,' he said to Mike when he'd finished.

'Ain't got more than a few dollars.'

'Hand it over,' the man said impatiently. 'I need every cent.'

When the Yuma man had checked he'd got all the money available from the men he walked over to the wagon. 'Need to move fast. Could sure use some trans-port but this wagon 'ud be easy to identify – and track.' He walked up front and eyed the mules. 'Mmm, ain't never rid a mule before.'

'And I shouldn't try now,' Mike said. 'Them critters ain't never been back-rid. Even if you could get on one, you wouldn't get far. More likely to end up with a broke bone or two. Be more trouble than it's worth.'

'Yeah,' Whelan huffed, 'you're right.' He gestured to the wagon. 'OK, last thing, I'm gonna need grub. What you got in the boot?'

When Mike had passed him a packet containing the remains of the food that Pat had prepared for them, the man looked into the trees. 'Well, thanks, fellers. You been real obliging.' And he was gone into the gloom.

For a few seconds the two men stared absently into the darkness, one still absorbing the complete surprise of the whole business, the other merely taken aback a tad at the unexpected turn in events.

'Well, what now, Mike?' Nahum said, his attempt at irony completely overwhelmed by the shivering that registered in his tone.

'First things first. It can get mighty cold out here at night so put Whelan's stuff on before you catch your death.'

'I ain't knowed you long,' Nahum said as he garbed himself in the prisoner's sackcloth, 'but thought I'd knowed you long enough to figure you were a straight guy. Well, I was sure wrong about that, wasn't I? Nothing to worry about, huh! That's a joke. And you told me another lie, Mike. You said this business wasn't nothing criminal.'

'I'm sorry it's worked out like this, Nahum, but I was real stymied. And Whelan pulling something like this was as much as surprise to me as to you. Wasn't in the deal.'

'What you on about? What deal?'

Mike dug in the breast pocket of his shirt and felt the comforting bulk of the Durham tobacco sack. 'Thanks be, Whelan didn't take my makings.'

'You're lucky; the bastard took mine.'

'Come on,' Mike said. 'Let's have a smoke.' He walked over to a knoll by the side of the track and plumped down. He worked to assemble the makings of a smoke, then handed the paraphernalia over to his comrade who had joined him.

The oldster rolled and firmed the paper around the tobacco strands and fitted the cigarette in the corner of his mouth. He struck a match to light on the heel of his boot, the brief sizzle of sound ringing unnaturally in the stillness.

'It's this way,' he said, speaking tightly around the butt of his smoke, cupping the match-flame to the tip until it flared and glowed alive. 'This gang of bozos turned up out of the blue in Rios a couple of days back. Cornered me in an alley and put me a proposition about getting timber to Yuma Pen. Offered good money too.'

'So? But what's that got to do with us springing Whelan out of the can?'

Mike took a fresh pull on his cigarette, blew a lazy trail of smoke that disappeared into the darkness. 'They'd done a bit of snooping. Been out to our place and spied on it. Done a little questioning in town. Knew all about me and Pat running the company.'

His slow delivery was irritating Nahum. 'What's all this got to do with me shivering my ass off in the middle of nowhere in a con's outfit?'

'Told me they aimed to use the delivery as a cover for getting one of their gang out of stir. That guy called Whelan. As leverage they said they would do unspeakable things to Pat if I didn't agree. Nahum, I was in a real spot.'

'Why didn't you say yes to get 'em off your back and then tell Sheriff Gallatin about it? He's seems a reasonable guy. The law could have handled it.'

The older man drew on his cigarette and grimaced as the acrid taste hit the back of this throat. 'They thought of that too. Said if I went to the law, it wouldn't stop 'em getting to Pat.' He grunted to add emphasis. 'I don't have to tell you the kind of things they were threatening with regard to what they would do to her.'

Nahum took the details in and sighed. 'So, like it or not, we're in it. What now?'

'Well, the plan was for us to take Whelan to meet up with his friends in a shack someways along this track. I've seen their signal – that lantern that I was looking for – so I got an idea where it is. The way I see it, only thing for it, I'm gonna have to go there and explain to them that he's skedaddled.'

'How they gonna take it?'

'God knows. But for Pat's sake I gotta try to get things straight with 'em.'

'And why do you think he's skedaddled?'

'Nahum, I've told you all I know. Why Whelan's not following the plan, I don't know. Your guess is as good as mine.' He ruminated for a moment. 'Listen, I think you should hold back. It was me that got involved in this mess. It's up to me to see it through. Ain't really your affair. I'll go up alone.'

'Oh, no, you don't. Now I understand the hole you've been in, I'm staying with you. From what you tell me, you don't know what you'll be riding into.'

'You sure?'

'You bet.'

'OK, come on. Let's git it over with.'

Back on the wagon, Mike flicked the ribbons and the mules resumed their struggle up the grade.

SEVEN

Somewhere up ahead of them a night-owl hooted, the sound carrying faint and ghostly in the stillness.

When the slope got steeper Mike reined in and soothed the fretting animals to quiet as the two men peered into the gloom. A dark mass of trees and rock answered their look. Further on, a ragged stretch of clearing cut a hole in their surroundings that let in the black night sky and the dazzling fire of its stars.

Mike rose up from his seat to get a better vantage point and looked to the east. 'Ha,' he said. 'Can see light again. Ain't too far. Marks a deserted mine, they told me. Shouldn't be long now.'

They'd travelled no more than another hundred yards into the murk when a voice boomed, 'Whoa there.'

Mike pulled in.

'Give a name, pilgrim.'

'Bill Sughrie. Sorry, pal, I mean Mike Tough.'

'You don't seem sure.'

'I'm sure. Mike Tough.'

A man with a rifle moved into the moonlight and

crossed to the wagon. A full-length grey slicker gave him a spectral appearance in the darkness. Mike recognized him as one of the gang who visited him in Rios. The man gestured to the vehicle with his weapon. 'That the merchandise?'

'There's been a problem.'

'Problem?' the man grunted. 'What kind of problem?'

'Best I tell your boss in person.'

'Please yourself. But whatever the problem is I don't think the chief's gonna like it.' He took the halter of the nearest mule and led the wagon on.

Rounding a bend in the track, the visitors glimpsed a lantern hanging high in a tree, and found themselves met by a far bigger clearing. A low plank- and log-timbered building came to sight in the open stretch, the area being fenced with a circle of rough-cut posts, their rotting shapes just discernible in the darkness. Their way was blocked by a high, barred gate behind which stood another light-slickered figure. A darting spasm of brightness told of moonlight striking a rifle barrel.

Seeing the advancing wagon, the second man moved forward. 'This 'em?'

'Yeah,' his colleague returned. 'Let us through, Eddie.'

The other hurried to the unfastening of rawhide clasps and heaved the creaking gate back on its hinges.

As the guard passed through the gateway, the man guiding the mules gestured towards the lantern. 'You can get that thing down from the tree now. No need to advertise our presence without due cause. When you've done that, stay out here on guard.'

The cart trundled past four horses tethered near the building. Down from their wagon the two freighters stepped up onto the weathered boards of the building from which a shingle hung loose, flapping a little in the slight, night wind. They were ushered inside where there were another two long-coated men basking in the light of oil-lamps.

Nahum's enquiring eyes took stock of each of the three men, noting the differing build of each: the one who had escorted them, tall and rawboned; standing to one side another, heavy-set; and seated in the middle, the third man thin and slight, with a foxy face and rusty hair.

'Ha, Mr Tough,' the foxy one said. 'About damn time.'

He looked more closely at Nahum in his prison garb. 'That's not Whelan,' he snapped. 'What's the game?' His gaze returned to Mike. 'You've got the wrong man, you bozo!'

'Old guy said there's been a problem, boss,' their escort put in.

'If they've sprung the wrong man,' the headman continued, 'you're damn right there's a problem.'

'Begging your pardon, mister,' Mike spluttered. 'I don't think we got the wrong man. A man designated as Whelan was delivered to us in the prison and we had no reason to doubt his identity. The guys got him into the wagon and we brung him out here just like we were supposed to. Everything went OK, but for some reason when we got to the bottom of the track he got the drop on us.' He thumbed backwards in the direction in which they had come up the slope. 'He took our weapons and the clothes of my friend here – then disappeared. My friend's dressed this way because he had to put on the

58

guy's prison clothes on account of the cold.'

'What do you mean – Whelan disappeared?'

Mike explained in more detail how the man had absconded.

'You were paid good money – to bring him here.'

'We weren't to know he would be hostile to the idea of being sprung, sir.'

'He wasn't hostile to being sprung – he was hostile to us getting our hands on him!'

Mike and Nahum exchanged quizzical glances.

'You said he was a member of your gang,' Mike posited. 'That it was a matter of getting one of your pals out of the pen.'

'Oh, yeah. He's a member of the gang all right. But some of us have got different agendas.'

'I don't know what you mean, sir.'

The man looked around his comrades. 'This pair might be in cahoots with him, don't you think, fellers?'

Mike shook his head. 'No, sir. That we most certainly are not. But I don't understand. You rode into Rios and asked me to help him escape. The way you put your proposition I did as you bid. What more could you ask?'

'Something's smelling here,' the boss said. 'You gonna tell us the truth?'

'I've told you the truth.'

The man cast his eye around the room. 'Wessels, get that rope. And you Hagan, pull over those chairs and then tie 'em up.'

'Yes, sir,' the big man said, his black eyes lighting up, denoting he relished the task ahead.

Nahum felt the rope go round him, and thought about trying something. The hard gaze of too many eyes dissuaded him, and he stayed quiet, hearing the man behind him grunt in effort as the knots were made fast, lashing him to the rickety chair. When the task was completed he looked to his side and saw Mike in the same predicament.

'Now,' the headman said, 'let's recap so things are in the open and there ain't no misunderstanding. Whelan and his sidekick Shaughnessy were members of our gang.'

'Shaughnessy?' Mike said. 'Ain't never heard of Shaughnessy. And only know of Whelan through this deal.'

'Yeah, Jimmy Shaughnessy, long-time pal of Whelan's. The two of 'em joined our outfit together some time back. Fitted in, kept their noses clean, never gave me any inkling they couldn't be trusted. Whelan, he was espe-cially useful. We weren't doing good for grub at the time and he told the tale that he'd been a cook on a riverboat so he conveniently took over our provisioning. Anyways, the two of 'em were with us when we knocked off a bank over in Kansas. We pulled a good haul and got clear too. Problem is Whelan and Shaughnessy had got ideas of their own. First meal Whelan cooked for us after the job, he slipped som'at into the hash. Don't know what the hell it was but it knocked us out for the best part of twenty-four hours. When we came to, Whelan and Shaughnessy had disappeared – along with fifty grand.'

He waved a finger taking in the circle of his compan-ions. 'Now me and the boys, we didn't take too kindly to that and set out to locate the varmints and recoup our funds. We tracked the renegade pair out here to Arizona. Guess they were aiming to lose themselves in the territory. But next thing we hear, Shaughnessy is dead and Whelan is charged with his murder. Looks like they had an argument, probably over the money.

'I've long come to the understanding that our Eugene Whelan is an all-round bad piece of work and the more I learn of him the more I figure he just wanted the funds all for hisself. That would explain why he would be prepared to kill a long-time pal. Anyways, that's how come Whelan was in Yuma Pen – got life for murder. Now there was no mention of the bank robbery or the money, when they collared him. So that means he's stashed it someplace. We've got our contacts and arranged for Whelan to be sprung from the can. Problem was, we didn't want to do it directly ourselves – our faces ain't known yet in these parts and we don't want 'em to be. For that reason we needed a stooge, somebody legitimate who'd got the means – and we picked on you.'

'This is all news to me,' Mike said.

'You probably noticed how easy it was to get Whelan out of the place,' Lyle went on. 'That's because all prison guards in proximity to Whelan had been bribed. Like I said, we got our contacts. So, my friend, we got a lot riding on this. The stolen cash, not to mention the resources we've put in, miscellaneous expenses and a mountain of greenbacks gone on bribes.'

The gang boss studied his captives. 'Whelan's stashed this fifty grand someplace and we intend to recover it. Now, seems to me, a potentially rich guy like Whelan could elicit help – from someone such as yourselves. He's in a position to promise a lot.'

'I've told you, I know nothing about what you've just

told me,' Mike said. 'And I know nothing about any hidden money.' He thought on it. 'Christ, would we come back to you if we were in cahoots with Whelan? Wouldn't make sense.'

'And what about your pardner here?' the man said.

'Leave the lad be,' Mike said. 'He knows nothing about this job apart from being paid to deliver timber to the prison. Even when we got there and Whelan was being smuggled into the wagon he didn't know what was going on. He only learned its nature when Whelan revealed himself in back of the wagon on the journey up here.'

'So what's he doing in all this?'

'Just works for us, a new boy. He was needed for this particular job, it being long distance and a heavy job calling for two guys. Listen, fellers, what I say is true. He's only been with our outfit a few weeks. He can't help you either.'

'I don't trust new boys. Whelan and Shaughnessy were new boys and look where that got me. New or old, there's some chance that he's seeking to feather his nest on a promise from Whelan.'

'No, mister,' Nahum butted in. 'I'm sure Mike don't know nothing about stolen money. And I sure as hell don't.'

The back of Hagan's big-boned hand struck him stingingly across the mouth, hard enough to rock his head sideways and draw blood. Nahum puckered and spat, tasting the salt of blood in his mouth and glowered at the heavy-set man who had delivered the blow. The cowpuncher had been in enough brawls in his time to make a good account of himself, even big guys like the one who was leering at him now.

'You yellow bonehead,' he growled. 'I'd like to see you try that when my hands were free.'

The bull of a man who had delivered the blow drew his heavy Colt. 'Why, you sassy bastard.'

Nahum saw the speaker's body tauten, clenching at the words. He caught a light that threatened back of the big man's black eyes, and braced himself for what was coming. The gun whipped down and slammed against the side of Nahum's head. The last thing he knew was the hard, numbing impact of metal against bone. And someone put the light out and everything went black.

'You damn fool, Hagan,' the leader snapped, eyeing the limp form. 'You and your ham-fisted ways. He's gonna talk a lot now, isn't he?'

'He was deliberately bugging me, boss.'

'There was no need for hitting him like that,' Mike wheezed. The old man was having trouble breathing. 'I've told you, he knows nothing.'

The chief turned his attention to the remaining conscious man. 'Never mind that. I don't want to hear nothing from you but the deal you struck with Whelan and where he's headed. You gonna tell us something useful?'

'I keep telling you, we're just ordinary working guys. I'll return the dough you paid me for the job if you give me a chance. I'd give you some now but Whelan took our cash down to our last cent before he vamoosed.'

'You try my patience, pilgrim.' The boss looked at the unconscious cowman, then back at Mike, and turned to the hefty one of his colleagues. 'We'll concentrate on the oldster for the time being. He's a mite frailer and should be easier to get talking. See what you can do, Hagan.'

The man struck Mike across the face. The old man's head zipped sideways with the blow and then slumped forward. Mike worked his jaw as blood dribbled from his lips. 'I'm telling you the truth, fellers.'

In the quiet of the moment that followed the chief took stock of the feeble figure. 'OK, at least you can tell us where Whalen was headed.' His voice bit hard as a bear-trap, green stare of his eyes cold in the freckled face.

'Last I saw he seemed to be heading back down the track,' Mike gasped, his words very slow, his face beginning to contort. 'Whether he made it to the main trail or turned off I don't know; it was near to pitch black.'

'You must have had some words with him before he lit out. He say anything about what he was up to, where he was going? Anything that might save you some pain?'

'No, sir. Nothing. Just took what he wanted then was gone.'

The foxy man reached inside the folds of his jacket, brought out a thin-stemmed cigarette. He stuck it in the corner of his mouth and struck a match with his thumb-nail. He lit up, his cold stare coming back to the old man.

'I still think you know more.' He drew on the cigarette and breathed the sweet-scented smoke in the face of the bound man as his hard voice whispered the words, 'To suffer a little more may be enough,' he added and nodded to the hefty man who slammed his fist into Mike's face again, knocking back his head.

This time the head stayed back. Then there was a groan, a long exhalation of breath and the figure went limp.

'Not another one passing out on us?' the chief muttered. 'For sweet Mary's sake, wake the old bastard up.'

The big man tapped at Mike's face a couple of times, one way then the other. He stepped back, appraised his work for a moment and shook the old man by the shoulders. He leant forward and put his ear to the bound man's mouth. 'Don't think he's gonna wake, boss,' he said in a surprised tone. 'Know what? Reckon he's cashed in his chips.'

The only emotion registering on the chief's face was frustration. 'Hell, what a hog's ass this is turning into.'

The bulky man looked across at the other hunched figure. 'Shall I douse some water over the tall guy, boss? Maybe we can get something out of him.'

The other shook his head. 'No. The more I look at him the more he looks nothing more than a simple paid hand. Reckon he knows even less.'

He exhaled noisily in irritation. 'Shite, we've wasted enough time. Hagan, see if you can do something bloody useful and get the hosses ready.'

He huffed again, then pulled himself to his feet. 'Come on, boys, let's get down to the main trail. See if we can track Whelan. It's dark but on foot he couldn't have got far.'

EIGHT

Nahum sat slumped in the chair, rising slowly to the halfway station between unconsciousness and awareness. He grimaced as he felt pain return as a white-hot spike at the side of his head. He became aware of the tightness of the rope across his chest, dryness in his mouth. Recent events started coming back. He waited for a few moments while consciousness slowly kicked in, then slowly opened his eyes. One of the lamps had burnt out but there was enough of a flicker from the other for him to see that Mike was in a bad way.

He stopped thinking about his own privations and called his friend's name. No response. The jaspers must have knocked the old man unconscious in the same way as he. He turned his head and listened. No sound anywhere but the slight wind through a broken window. Had the gang gone?

It took a long time – he didn't know how long – to work himself free. Shucking the coils he staggered over to the old man.

'Jesus,' he breathed when he felt for pulses and found none. In a kind of panic he worked at the man's flesh but he noticed there was a distinct coolness to it. The old fellow was not only dead but must have been so for a good while.

'Then how long have I been out?' he questioned himself.

Cautiously he went outside. The gang's horses had gone. It was still dark but he thought he could discern a glow on the underbelly of clouds to the east. If so, dawn was approaching.

He looked around. The mules and wagon were still there. Either the jaspers had had no use for them or had left in a hurry.

Back inside the shack he unticd Mike's body and laid it gently on the floor. He contemplated the figure for a while. He hadn't known the old guy for very long, but long enough to get to like him.

'Oh, Mike,' he breathed. 'You poor guy. Why did it have to turn out like this?'

He sighed and, still in a daze, slumped in a chair. 'What next?'

Pulling himself together he made a search of the building but found nothing useful, nothing that gave him any ideas.

Outside it was getting lighter. He found a well with the vestiges of water from which he chanced a few distasteful sips, then used to freshen his face. He watered the mules and stood in the middle of the yard pushing things around his mind. His first thought was to bury his employer, then decided it more proper to take the body home as he still had the means in the shape of the wagon.

It wasn't until he'd laid his friend in the wagon that he

realized he had a long way yet to go and was not likely to get far dressed in prison clothes.

'I know you wouldn't mind,' he said as he removed Mike's over-clothes. 'You won't miss 'em now anyways.'

When he had completed the unpleasant task he climbed aboard and flicked the ribbons to begin the descent down the rough track. Reaching the main trail he pointed the wagon towards Rios.

Luckily he'd remembered the meanderings of the outward journey from Rios and finally made the town just as it was getting dark. He made his way through the main drag and out to the company's place on the other side of town.

He knocked the door and pushed it open. A sewing basket at her side, Pat was mending a pair of Levis.

'God, what's happened?' she said, leaping out of her seat and crossing to the bedraggled figure in the doorway. 'You look awful. I been worried. You were so long.'

'Got some bad news, Pat. Mike's dead.'

'What? Dead? An accident?'

'No, it's complicated.'

'Where is he?'

'I'll get a lamp.'

She was crying uncontrollably by the time he had taken her outside and pulled back the tarp.

'It's a dreadful mess, Pat.'

They were sitting against the fireplace with shot glasses full of whiskey. While they had carried Mike's body and laid it on the bed, he'd given her the bare bones of events, for the moment skimming over precise details.

'Apparently it all started when a band of bank-robbers turned up in Rios,' he explained when they were back downstairs. 'They paid Mike a visit.'

'I didn't see them. He didn't tell me.'

'No, he wouldn't because they wanted him to help get one of their number out of the pen.'

'He wouldn't have had anything to do with something like that. He was as straight as they come.'

'Wasn't that simple.'

'Then why would he comply?'

Nahum paused for a moment, hesitant to say how the focus had been on Pat, then concluded it was best that she knew. 'Fact is, they threatened to harm you, Pat. They meant it. I've seen 'em. They're evil men.'

She closed her eyes and slumped her head. 'So he did it for me.'

'There are four of the critters. The leader was a short, foxy-faced feller. One of 'em, the one I figure killed Mike, was a large bull of a guy. You say you didn't see any sign of them?'

'No.'

'Anyway, that was the Yuma job. Wasn't about delivering timber at all. You never guessed there was something odd about the deal?'

'No. But now you've told me of these things it does occur to me that Mike was a mite secretive about it. And explains how come the job was being extra well paid.' She shook her head. 'Huh, when I pressed him he put on a show, winking and saying it wasn't what you know but who you know. I understand now he was doing his best to shield me from the truth.' Thoughtfully she took a slow drink from her glass. 'So that's what it was all about.'

69

'Yeah.' Nahum paused as he kicked things around in his mind. 'We gotta consider what to do next. The more I think about it, Pat, the more I reckon it's best we keep the truth under wraps. I'm sure Mike thought he was acting for the best but it ain't gonna serve any purpose by making the whole thing public.'

'You're right. Then there's you. Although we know you're really innocent of any conniving, the truth could cause you a heap of trouble.'

He grunted. 'Yeah. I've pondered on that likelihood myself.'

'Getting down to practicalities,' she said, 'They'll track the matter to us. They'll know the company name. Slaughter and Tough, it'll be on the prison's paperwork with regard to the timber. That'll bring them straight here!'

'No. Mike had thought about that. Used a fictitious name. Even went to the lengths of having a false bill printed on the quiet someplace. He'd done his homework all right. He worked out a false name for me too.'

'Mmm. There's still the gang and their search for the missing cache. You said they thought that you and Mike might know where it is. Think they'll turn up here again?'

'Don't think so. Mike's dead – he won't be able to help them anymore – and I figure they accepted the notion I don't know anything.'

He thought about it some more. 'Anyways, first thing, we got to do the decent thing by Mike. I mean Christian burial and all.'

'Of course.'

'I think we should wait until morning, then call the

doc and say we came across Mike in the barn when we noticed that his bed hadn't been slept in. We'll say we found him lying at the foot of the ladder, looking like he fell from the loft section. That might explain the damage to his face.'

She considered Nahum's face 'And how do we explain *your* bruising? That's quite a bump on your temple.'

He thought about it. 'Yeah, might be awkward if the doc sees the state I'm in. Might start asking tricky questions.' Then, 'Tell you what, you see the doc alone. Say I'd already gone out on an early job by the time you had found Mike's body.' He felt the tender part of his head again. 'Then I'll keep out of the limelight till this thing heals over a bit.'

'That reminds me,' she said. 'Come into the kitchen and I'll bathe it.'

'Yes,' the doctor said when he'd examined the body laid out on the bed the following morning. 'Signs are consistent with a heart attack. His ticker had been of concern for some time.'

'I didn't know,' Pat said.

'Fellers sometimes keep these things to themselves, miss. He'd seen me a couple of times about pains. I gave him some elixir, told him to slow down, to rest more. That's all I could do. Suppose he didn't tell you about these things.'

'No.'

'Well, for completeness, show me where you found him.'

She took him into the barn and pointed to the foot of the ladder. 'He was crumpled there.'

'Yes,' he concluded after an appraisal. 'As to the facial bruising we can surmise that he fell during the spasm and suffered the injury on impact at the bottom.' He looked up to the loft. 'It's quite a distance from there to the ground. Poor Mike.'

They returned outside.

'When I get back to town,' he said, as he settled back on his buggy, 'I'll arrange for the funeral parlour to collect the deceased. You want that I should I notify the priest about the funeral at the same time?'

'No, thanks. I feel it's my duty to arrange all those matters personally.'

'Of course. I understand. I know you were close.' He gave a final touch of his hat. 'My condolences, Miss Slaughter.'

'Ashes to ashes, dust to dust.'

The funeral was two days later at the cemetery on the low hill outside the town. Mike had been an established and popular figure in the locality, so the occasion was well attended.

Pat and Nahum stood at the graveside where the fresh-turned dust beside it was already drying out and cracking in the morning heat.

There had been some improvement in the damage to Nahum's face but it still showed and he would have chosen not to attend, but the couple debated the matter and came to the conclusion that his absence might have created some suspicion.

Handfuls of soil were thrown on the box. Pat dabbed her eyes as they stepped away and the gravedigger began to complete the filling in. When he'd finished she laid a handful of flowers that she had plucked that morning. But the sun was already shrivelling them, and they looked pale and sickly on the heap of dirt.

She shook hands with the priest, thanked him and moved slowly towards the gate with Nahum alongside.

She was still sobbing when Sheriff Gallatin stepped in their path a few paces beyond the cemetery.

He took off his hat. 'My sympathies, Miss Slaughter.'

'Thank you, Sheriff.'

He returned the hat to his head. 'I'm sorry to intrude at such a time, miss, but I have some business with Mr Crabtree here.'

'What can I do for you, Sheriff?' Nahum said slipping on his own hat. 'And you can call me Nahum.'

'Can you and I speak in private?'

'I got nothing to hide from Miss Slaughter. Anything you got to say to me can be said in front of the lady.'

'Very well. Fact is, Nahum, I'm afraid I'm gonna have to ask you to come with me.'

'Why?'

'Got an odd telegraph message from the sheriff's office in Yuma. He's working with the prison authorities out there. There's been a prison break and' – he made a humourless grunt – 'you ain't gonna believe this but they say they've got a description of a Slaughter & Tough's company wagon. Say it was involved and last seen heading out this way. Two guys were manning it. You know anything about this?'

Man and woman mouthed a simultaneous 'no'.

'I thought not. I told 'em I ain't never heard of your outfit working out that-a-ways – Yuma's right out of your neck of the woods – but it didn't wash. On top of that, for the life of me, can't see how they can tell one wagon from another. Anyways, we'll have to see. Upshot is, they've requested I detain Nahum until they can get over here to question him.'

'This is unbelievable,' Pat said.

'Yeah, that's what I think,' the lawman said. 'I know the sheriff out there. He's a good guy and I'm sure it'll sort itself out, miss, but at this stage it's outa my hands, you understand. Much as it's against my wishes I gotta comply with their request, otherwise I could be deemed as obstructing the course of justice and that could give me a whole can of trouble. So if you can accompany me to the law office, Nahum.'

'Sure thing, Sheriff. Anything to help clear up this thing.'

'Don't know how long I'm gonna have to detain you. You need to fetch anything before we go?'

'No. I can come as I am.'

'You live over at the company house now, I hear,' the lawman said.

'Yeah.'

'So, if there's anything you need I'm sure Miss Slaughter will bring it over to the office.' He looked at the woman. 'Feel free to come over any time, miss.'

Nahum clutched Pat's hand briefly before turning to leave. 'Don't fret. Everything's gonna be OK.'

Then, as the two men walked away the sheriff turned. 'That's right, miss. Don't worry. As I've said I'm sure there's an acceptable explanation. Meantimes, I'll see that Nahum's stay is as comfortable as I can make it.'

NINE

The jail was a small place, the main function of its single cell being to give the occasional drunk somewhere to sober up. Rios was that peaceable sort of town.

Nahum lay on the bunk pondering on his circumstances. He had given himself up with no argument for several reasons; because there'd been nothing to be gained by doing otherwise; because he'd been caught unawares; and because he had been raised to be a law-abiding citizen and you complied with law officers.

But the more he thought about it the blacker things looked. If he told the truth to those whose job it was to judge, if he admitted he was one of those aiding the prisoner to escape but had done so innocently, there was only his word. The authorities had no reason to believe him. He was a stranger in town, an unknown quantity. And the one person who could clear him was now below dirt in Rios cemetery. If he denied outright going on the job, he might find himself facing witnesses able to identify him. Caught in one lie, he'd have less of a leg to stand on in his claim of innocence.

What was the sentence for aiding a prisoner to escape?

He had no idea but he guessed a long term.

And it hadn't taken the sheriff long to take a close look at his captive's face while installing him in the cell. The officer could do nothing but accept the cowman's explanation that he had fallen against a wagon while loading it. But Nahum recalled the quizzical look that had remained on the man's face at the end of the exchange.

His thoughts were interrupted by the unlocking of the outer door. It was Sheriff Gallatin bearing a piece of paper that he brought to the cell. 'Message just in from Yuma. They'll be coming to collect you tomorrow.'

'Good,' Nahum said in acknowledgement, putting on a front that he had little concern about the matter other than its inconvenience. 'The sooner this thing is over the better. I been thinking, with Mike gone there's only Pat left over at the freightyard and it's gonna be hard for her alone. Fact is, can't see her doing much at all. Business is probably grinding to a standstill already.'

'I been thinking about things. You know, Mike going the way he did and all. Real odd, something happening to him at this time. And that messing up of your face. You sure there ain't no connection between these things?'

'Don't see your meaning, Sheriff. What connection could there be?'

The sheriff returned to his front office leaving Nahum to realize that in his answer he had already started digging the lying pit.

A little after noon, Pat brought him lunch. The town being a small, tight community, the sheriff had known her since she was young and, as he had promised, he allowed her unhindered access to the cell.

The couple talked while Nahum ate. He told her about the imminent arrival of the Yuma men. She was concerned, but he tried to allay her worries and when he had finished eating she took away the dirty dishes.

With a full stomach and nothing to do but wait he dozed off prompted by the confined heat of the small building.

He awoke later in the afternoon, his mind in turmoil. Mysteriously the name Tyler was coming up from somewhere. He didn't know anybody with such a name so why should it come to the surface like this? Following the blow in the shack his recall of events had been patchy but bits were coming back. Not much but enough to know he had some kind of talk with Whelan during the short period they had been alone. But he couldn't remember details. His brow furrowed as he trawled the recesses of his mind. Maybe this Tyler guy had something to do with that.

What he did know is that he had developed a strong urge to get out of the place. Maybe because, as an outdoor man, he had never been cooped up for so long before; maybe because some unknown thing was driving him. He didn't know. But something was making him real antsy.

As he listened to the sheriff pottering about in the front room, Nahum looked around his cell. It hadn't been constructed to hold hardened criminals; just drunks. Surely a determined fellow whose brain wasn't stewed in alcohol could work some way out of the place. From where he was lying on the cot the most likely weak element in his confinement was the door. He dearly wished to give it a closer inspection but that part of the

77

cell was in clear sight of the front office and vigilant sheriff.

All he could do was wait and think. His patience was rewarded when the sheriff was called away on business. From what he heard it wouldn't be for long, so Nahum would have to work quickly. As soon as the front door closed behind the lawman, he leapt up. The cell door hung on simple hinges about three inches long. He breathed deep and heaved. It was real heavy but he could raise the whole thing about an inch. Not enough.

He looked up at the ceiling directly above it. Like the rest, it was crude planking. If the piece running above the top of the door could be removed, or chipped away significantly, maybe he could raise the pivot side of the door another two inches, thereby allowing it to clear the hinges completely.

He thought about it. Looked possible. All he needed was some tools. The hours of darkness would be the time to do it. At that time, with the sheriff sleeping off the premises at night, a little noise should present no problem.

When Pat brought him a snack late afternoon he engaged her in inconsequential talk for a while. Towards the end of the meal he beckoned for her to lean forward and he whispered, 'Listen, would you mind helping me? I mean really help me?'

She made to speak but he touched her lips with his finger. 'I want you to bring some things with my supper,' he said in a barely audible voice.

She gestured compliance.

'You remember our dear sheriff said you could bring

me anything I needed?' he asked with a wry smile.

'Yes.'

'Well, I could do with a small hammer and chisel.'

Momentary lack of understanding showed in her furrowed brow.

He rose and threw a checking glance toward the front room. Noting that the sheriff was seated with his back to him, he silently indicated the planking above the door and mimed the action of chipping the wood.

Back beside her he whispered against her ear, 'Understand?' and repeated his mime.

She nodded.

He could tell she was bursting with questions but once again he placed his finger on her lips.

'That was a splendid meal,' he said loudly, winking.

It was midnight. It had been half an hour since the sheriff had emptied his prisoner's bucket, asked him if he was OK for the night and left. Moonlight and the low-lit lamp in the front office were enough for him to see all he wanted. The sliver of plank was easy to fetch out with the chisel needing very little use of the hammer in the event.

He couldn't raise the door on the lock side very far on account of the locking bar but, exerting all his strength, he could manage to lift the other side just enough to clear the hinges. Then all he had to do was swing that side of the door towards him, enabling him to slip the fastening bar out of the lock. He laid the heavy door down as quietly as he could. In the front office he collected his gunbelt and other belongings. Both front and back doors were locked but there was an assortment of keys hanging from hooks for him to choose from, and he soon found the one to the back door. Leaving from the rear kept him clear of the main street, and he loped through the night air towards the freightyard.

Pat hugged him when he made his appearance. 'Did anyone see you?'

He smiled. 'No. That's another reason why I'm glad this is a quiet go-to-bed-at-night town. Nobody about at all.'

'What are your plans? Do you want to hide out here?'

He shook his head. 'That'd be crazy. This is the first place the sheriff would think of.'

'Maybe, but there's a heap of hidey holes around the place where you could hide.'

'And none of them secure when the prison authorities turn up in town later today and soon come here to go through it with a toothcomb. They're professionals at this game. No, I gotta get out of town completely.'

'OK, but where you gonna go?'

'Dunno.' He thought about it. 'Figure the only chance I got of beating this rap is to catch Whelan and take him in myself. Kinda redress the balance. Maybe that'll put me in a good light with the law.'

She shook her head in disbelief. 'Talk about long shots. How you going to do that?'

'I'm gonna have to assume the gang didn't catch him back near that shack up in the hills. I have to, it's my only hope.'

'But how you gonna track him?' she asked. 'Have you got any experience in tracking and that kind of thing?'

'I've had to root out stray steers in my day.'

'I don't want to be a wet blanket, Nahum, but there's

a world of difference between tracking a lost steer that's wandered a mile or so away from the herd and tracking a man over half the country.'

What she said was true. He remained quiet.

'It's a hard thing for me to suggest,' she offered, 'but now that you've broken out of custody I figure the only course for you to take is change your name and get yourself lost someplace for good. Start a new life.'

'Ain't doing that.'

'Why not? Can't see any other options if you don't want to spend a goodly proportion of your young life in Arizona's leading penitentiary.'

He took both her hands in his, holding them as though she might have broken away from him. 'For a start, Pat, I don't want to leave you.'

'What do you mean?'

'Ever since I've been here in Rios I've been thinking about you. I mean all the time.'

She touched his cheek, almost disbelievingly. 'I had no idea. You were always so . . . offhand.'

'The way I am, I reckon.'

He stroked her hands, his range-calloused skin contrasting with the relative softness of hers. 'I gotta tell you, Pat, you're the best thing that's happened to me. Just being in your presence. Sitting with you at your table, eating the food you've cooked with these hands, talking with you, passing the evening with you. I go up to my room at night and can't get you out of my mind. My head close to the pillow and sheets that you clean with your own hands. The smell of you when you're close. It's a helluva time to tell you but I declare you're the purtiest female I've ever set eyes on. Pat, this feeling I got, I've never known anything like it. It's something . . . something I've never knowed before.'

She nestled her head against him. 'Oh, Nahum.'

He raised his hands. 'And now all this . . . fandango. If only there had been a way for Mike to have handled it differently.'

'Water under the bridge. Now we've got to think of what happens next.'

'I've had an idea. A slim one but something.'

'What's that?'

'You know, I've been knocked out before, getting stunned after falling from a horse, that sort of thing. Not a rarity in my line out on the range. But when those guys in that shack whammed me, the blacking out was a heap worse. Ain't experienced anything like it. Even when I came to, for a time everything had gone; I couldn't remember a lot of things that had happened: where I was and why. I've still been a mite hazy about what happened immediately before that bozo whopped me with his gun. But slowly things have been coming back. I kept trying to remember the conversation I had with Whelan during the short while Mike went scouting ahead. I kept feeling there might be something useful there.'

He thumbed in the direction of town. 'Then back in the jail, more came back. I can remember that Whelan asked me if I knew somebody. Then it came to me: Tyler, that was the name. He wanted to know if I knew Tyler. Now if I can locate this guy, I might be getting someplace. Any ideas?'

'Could have been a gang-member.'

'Don't think so. If Whelan was aiming to evade them, he wouldn't be interested in contacting one of them.'

'That doesn't follow. From what you told me this Shaughnessy sidekick of Whelan's was a gang-member too, and *he* double-crossed them.'

'Yeah, it could be there was another member of the gang involved with him.' He paused. 'Still, on second thoughts, no. The men back at that shack didn't mention Tyler as a doublecrosser. And, if he was one of their mob, they would have known about him, like they knew about Shaughnessy. They would have brung up the name when they were questioning me and Mike. No, I figure this Tyler is somebody outside the gang, maybe someone who is involved with Whelan in the doublecross.' He paused. 'But then, would he be likely to have revealed the name to me? Oh hell, I don't know.'

He thought about things and the doubts that kept surfacing in his mind caused his brow to crease. 'Pat, I wonder if I'm doing the right thing here.'

'Now you've committed yourself, there's no going back. By breaking out of jail you've compounded whatever trouble you're already in. So, most important thing is for you to light out as soon as possible. It'll give you time to think. You can take Mike's saddle horse. Come on, rouse yourself. Then, while you're getting ready, I'll put together some food and fill a couple of canteens with water.'

He looked sheepish. 'If I'm going, I need yet another favour, Pat. I sure hate to ask but I'm gonna need some money too.'

'Nahum, you can have everything I got in the house. Whatever I can scrape up you're welcome to.'

He hugged her. 'Pat, you're an angel.'

'I could get more tomorrow from the bank. There's

83

not a great deal in the account but whatever there is yours for the asking.'

'That would be cutting it fine. Thanks for the thought but can't wait that long.'

He had brought Mike's dun stallion round the back of the house where it was out of sight of the approach road. He was tightening the cinch when Pat bounced out of the back door.

'It's just occurred to me. You spoke as though Tyler was a man. But do you think Tyler might be a *place*, not a man?'

'What do you mean? A place? Where?'

'Don't know. But I reckon I've heard of such a place. Can't say when and where. You know, one of those vague things lodged at the back of one's mind.'

'Any idea where it might be?'

'Never been, so got no clue of its whereat – if it exists. But I've got this hazy notion there's such a place. Feeling it might be to the north.' She scratched her head. 'Can't be more precise than that.'

He grabbed and kissed her. 'You're a darling! That's the first glimmer of something I've had to go on.' He thought on it. 'Hey, if it's a place it could be where Whelan's heading. Might even be where he's stashed the dough!'

She pulled herself away. 'Don't get too excited. It's only an idea. I might be completely wrong.'

'You got a map?'

'Of course. It's indispensable in our line.'

Minutes later the crumpled chart was unfolded on the dining table and they were running their fingers over its surface. It was Pat who found it. Her finger jabbed at the word. 'There – Tyler!'

He spanned the distance with his thumb and little finger. 'About sixty miles from Rios,' he concluded, glancing at the scale. 'Something like that. Should be able to get there.'

Then he looked at her. 'Pat, the more I think about it, the more I'm worried about you being implicated.'

She shrugged, dismissing the notion. 'Even if some-body can identify the Slaughter & Tough wagon like they're claiming, there were two *men*. No woman involved. I have no connection with Whelan or the bank-robbers, so no motive. And I really doubt if they can identify a wagon as ours with any certainty anyway.'

'And your helping me out of jail? That could cause you a problem.'

'How can they tie me in with that?' she said with a calming smile. 'You brought the tools back. Can't tie me in with that either. No proof. They can only speculate. Don't worry. I'm going to be all right.'

'You sure?'

'I've told you not to worry,' she said, rising. 'Nearly got your stuff together,' she added, and disappeared at a dash into the kitchen.

On his horse, finally prepared, he leant forward from the saddle and kissed her very gently on the forehead. 'Pat, if ever I get out of this chowder . . .'

'I'll be here,' she whispered with a tightness in her throat.

Her hand trembled in his for a moment, then he was gone.

TEN

The dun stallion picked its way through the fly-blown heaps left by dogs and horses along the main drag of Tyler. Although not much more than fifty miles, without precise directions and no knowledge of the region, it had taken Nahum the best part of the day to reach the town. The wood that fronted the buildings was warped and weathered, old paint flaking. Out and beyond, the town seemed to drop away altogether, hindward side of the stores on to a spavined sprawl of brush windbreaks, and lean-to shacks, and after that nothing at all. Beyond, Arizona stretched away as far as the eye could see.

He soon found a saloon. Exhausted and dry, he needed something to wet his throat, then a place to lay his head. He pushed through the panelled batwings, battered and worn thin from all the drinkers who'd shoved their way through over the years. He took a drink and asked after a room. They'd got a place upstairs and he took it, booking in under the name of Jim Burnell.

It was a day later. Not wishing to arouse suspicions he'd

asked no questions and thankfully none had been asked of him. Within twenty-four hours, by simply hanging around, he reckoned he'd seen every inhabitant of the God-forsaken place – and none that looked liked Whelan. However, in the last regard he was wrong but didn't know it yet.

His mind was on what to do next. He'd drawn a blank on the only lead he had. Maybe there was another Tyler; maybe he had misheard the name. Maybe it had been a wild goose chase, maybe Pat had been wrong and Tyler was a feller after all, not a place.

He'd done all he could to pick up a clue. Over drinks he'd watched the folk in the saloon. From a chair on the boardwalk he'd kept his eye on the comings and goings. He'd sat at his bedroom window overlooking the street and done the same. Nothing.

Frustrated and restless, he went to the general store to pick up some supplies. Inside, he stood behind an old fellow who was purchasing coffee.

He was a thin, rawhide-tough little stump of a feller, like some of those trees out on the prairie, all bent and twisted from the storms and winds but still standing. Nahum had seen him before during his long day of vigil. But now standing close behind him with nothing else to do he noticed for the first time the fellow's vest. Made of leather it was too large across the man's shoulders but the length, especially short so as not to hamper working in the saddle, was not out of place on the small frame.

One thing Nahum knew: it was his very own! The one that had clothed his back since before he could remember. The one he had been wearing on the Yuma job when Whelan was looking for a change of clothing and demanded he strip. No doubt it was his, right down to the horseshoe burn on the side, a reminder of what could have been a nasty accident many years ago round a branding fire. During the years he had worn it, the vest had pinched his shoulders but it had served its purpose. Contrariwise, it sat well on the little man. Yes, it was his all right.

When it came to Nahum's turn at the counter he made do with a refill of tobacco so as not to arouse suspicion and returned to the street as quickly as possible – just in time to see the old fellow heading to the end of town. Nahum followed him, adopting a casual amble and keeping enough distance so that he could keep the man in view. Eventually his objective disappeared into a small house on the outskirts.

Did the vest connect Whelan to this place? Was this where the renegade had come to? The dwelling was neat with a plot of grass surrounded by flowers and a low picket fence. Suggested the touch of a woman. Keeping his distance, he slowly circled the building but saw no evidence of anyone other than the old man. He closed in to one wall and listened at an open window. He could hear someone pottering about, he guessed in the kitchen, but heard no voices. After a while he returned to the front and walked up the path.

His fingers close to his gun butt ready for anything, he stepped up onto the porch area and knocked at the door.

When the man answered, Nahum looked beyond him into the interior. When he was sure there was no one in proximity he said, 'Hope I ain't inconveniencing you, sir.'

'Might be. But what can I do for you?'

Nahum pointed to the vest and said, 'You might find this a rum observation for a stranger to make, but that burn on the right of that leather waistcoat was caused by its wearer helping a guy brand a calf and the iron slipped.'

The man's eyes widened.

'And,' Nahum continued, 'that scuffing on the left – that resulted from a guy falling from his hoss onto a mess of barb-wire.'

The man looked down at the vest and back at his visitor. 'Well, mister, I ain't got all day and I still don't understand why you come a-knocking on my door.'

'I'm saying I know those things because I'm that feller. Those things happened to me – showing that the vest is an old one of mine and I'm wondering how you came by it.'

'Hell, younker, it's mine!'

'OK, I ain't arguing. I just want to know how it came into your possession, is all.'

The man weighed his visitor up and down. Then said, 'You got time for a story, pilgrim?'

Nahum shrugged. 'You were polite enough to listen to me. Guess I can return the courtesy.'

The man stepped outside, plumped down in one of two chairs on the porch and indicated for his visitor to take the other.

'Don't see why I shouldn't tell you. Ain't nothing the rest of the town don't know.' He took out a gnarled cherrywood pipe. 'It's this way,' he went on, as he began to fill the thing from a pouch. 'My old woman was a treasure. We came out when we wus young and had a good life

89

here. Good times, bad times, but no complaints.'

He completed filling the pipe and stuffed it in his mouth. 'Then two years last fall the old dear went down with som'at. Out of the blue. Doc couldn't identify it.'

He lit a match and spent a while sucking, not satisfied until he was surrounded by voluminous clouds of smoke, much to the irritation of his impatient visitor.

'Anyways, the Good Lord took her within ten days. There I was, the centre of my life gone. I moped around for a spell, did some serious drinking, then I saw this advertisement: company out East offering wives. I didn't pay it much mind at the time. I was loath to even contemplate such an idea. Felt it was defiling the memory of my old gal. Then – would you believe it? – she came to me in a dream! As large as life, God rest her soul.'

Nahum fought growing impatience but hid the battle, not wanting to alienate the old man who had put out an exploring hand as though to touch his late wife.

'Just like she was standing real close to me,' the fellow continued. 'And she spoke! Said how she hated to see me so lonely, how she would understand if I sought feminine company. She was right on that count. A feller does miss the company of a woman, you know. And here she was, giving me the go-ahead! So I got myself some paper and scrawled out a letter to the company in the advertisement. I ain't too good at my letters but I managed it. Back comes a letter. I just had to send some dough – and Rachel turns up. Not the prettiest gal you ever saw but a pleasant sort and much younger than me.'

He winked. 'You know, firm flesh and all. Well, we seemed to get on, the age difference didn't seem to count for anything so we wed. After all, that's what the bargain was all about.'

He pointed along the street. 'Over in the chapel there. Well, for a spell things were OK. She cooked and tended to me. But then she got antsy. I understood that, you know. Reckon things out here were a sight quieter than she was used to. Huh, then she started disappearing for a few hours at a time. At first she was very mysterious about it but it wasn't long before I guessed what was going on and that she might be seeking the company of younger guys. In time she was staying out all night. That was just the start of her shenanigans. Things got worse. These fellers would call for her during the day! Worse still, she started flaunting her young men. You know, openly in front of me, ridiculing me for my age, that sort of thing. Women can be cruel.'

Getting more impatient, Nahum waved a finger vaguely at the man's chest. 'And what about the vest?'

'Well, this guy turns up out of the blue few days back – some no-account drifter – and she latches onto him real special. He buys her things, makes a fuss of her. Next thing I know she tells me she's leaving with him. Says she's sorry but she's found the love of her life. I mean, how can you tell something like that about a person within a couple of days? Then – whoosh – she's gone. Took a bunch of my money too. Virtually all of it. Left a note saying she was taking it because I owed her. When she vamoosed I had words with the sheriff about her helping herself to my dough. But he said it was a domestic matter so he couldn't do nothing. Out of his jurisdiction, he says.'

'And the vest?' Nahum pressed.

'Well, the woman-stealing bozo kitted them both out

in new duds. Dress for her and real swank clothes he
bought for hisself. Like they wus getting married or
something; only they can't get hitched on account she's
already married, can she?' He jerked a finger back to the
house. 'Left his old duds here, including this vest. And
that's how come I'm wearing it.'

'What was the guy's name?'

'Called hisself Brad Carter.'

The name was a new one to Nahum. 'You say that like
you don't believe him.'

'Sure as hell don't.'

'Why not?'

'Cos he'd got the same looks as the guy who he had
been staying with since he'd come to town. So much so,
they just gotta be kin. I reckon brothers.'

'And who's the guy he was staying with?'

'Sean Whelan.'

Nahum grunted in recognition on hearing the name,
then asked, 'This Sean Whelan, he been here long?'

'Oh, yeah. Maybe five seasons. Keeps the saloon.
You'll have seen him if'n you been in there.'

Nahum nodded. 'I been in there.'

'Now *he*'s a regular guy,' the old man continued. 'I got
time for him. The kind of guy you can pass the time of
day with, you know. It's his damn brother I don't like.
Funny thing, all the time this feller who calls hisself
Carter was staying at the saloon, he never came down for
a drink. Must be on the wagon or something.'

Or didn't cotton to being seen too much, Nahum
thought. Aloud, he said, 'This guy you think was the
saloonman's brother, you seen him before?'

'No.'

92

Nahum pointed to his right eyebrow. 'He got a scar here? Right down the middle. You know, splitting his eyebrow.'

The old man thought back. 'Now you mention, yeah. Knife slash or something like that.'

Nahum mused on what he had heard. He could see the plan. Visiting his brother would give Whelan somewhere to hole up for a short spell. *That*'s why he had been so keen to locate the town of Tyler. If Sean was the regular guy the old man figured, and keeping a saloon for five years suggested he was legitimate, he probably didn't even know his long-lost brother was on the run. Spouting some sob story, there was a strong chance Whelan had turned up wanting some money from him. Plus, he wouldn't want to stay too long as he was aiming to get to his big money cache. Nahum thought some more. Yes. The renegade would know that the gang as well as the law would be after him – and toting some besotted girl on his arm would provide good cover.

'What kinda duds did he garb himself out in?'

'Stuff from Chicago. Black hat and one of them Prince Albert coats. Big black thing, like I told yuh, real swank stuff.'

It figured: dignified clothing would add to his cover.

The old man thumbed his vest. 'And how did Carter come by this, this article that you claim was yours?'

'Oh, some dispute a while back. Nothing serious. Don't concern yourself with it, friend. You can keep it.' Nahum stood up. 'One last thing, when the couple left where were they heading?'

'No problem. Went out on the stage. Route's only got one destination: Allenville.'

'Well, much obliged. You been a help. Like I said, it intrigued me how come you were wearing my old vest, is all.'

'Glad to be of service.'

Nahum made to leave. 'One extra favour: I'd be appreciative if you didn't tell anyone about our little chat, especially the saloonkeeper.' Winking, he leant over and pushed a bill into the vest pocket.

'Anything you say, pilgrim,' the man said, touching his nose. 'Just between you and me.'

Within half an hour Nahum was on his way out of town.

How long it had taken him to come this far was something he didn't care to remember. From Tyler to Allenville had been a man-size stretch, and once he had landed there the stay had worn a bigger hole in Pat's grubstake. But he had learnt that Whelan and the girl had been there sure enough. Talk in the saloons and dives on the wrong side of town had told of the fancy-dressed dude and his companion, and how the fellow had managed to lose money at poker and faro tables. Seemed they'd left town and headed into the open country further north.

And there was a bonus. The fellow's losing at the tables meant he was short of cash. That could be good news. Problems were encumbrances. The more problems Whelan had, the easier he might be to catch up with.

94

ELEVEN

He had no experience in tracking but so far that deficiency hadn't mattered. The signs of two horses leaving Allenville had been plain. The unpopulated country of loose sand and dirt was like a school slate with horse prints and dung laid out as clearly as drawn chalk letters. Even the weather had made no attempt to remove the signs.

But he knew his luck wouldn't hold out forever and it didn't. The first signal was a dust cloud on the horizon. Even from a great distance he was familiar with its characteristics enough to know what it meant: a herd. A big one, too. And its crossing of the tracks that he was following would obliterate them. As he approached, his spirits fell further. He wouldn't put much of a bet on picking up the meagre sign of a pair of horses after the passage of such a mass. There'd be no trace.

Up close he recognized the breed: Herefords. But that useless observation was no compensation.

He looked at the sun to get his bearings. The only thing he could do was to maintain the same course and hope that the drive veered off out of his way, then try to pick up some sign of horse tracks on the far side. Huh, as if there was much chance of that.

He kept his horse at the same pace as the cattle, the dust hitting his nostrils reminding him of his own days as a 'puncher. Occasionally he would see a drover and they would exchange waves. Half an hour on and there was no indication that the herd was going to change direction.

His morale at rock bottom, he urged the dun onward.

'Well I'll be. That ain't Nahum, is it?'

His head was down, he had become oblivious of his surroundings, letting the dun take its head. He shook himself out of the semi-daze and turned in the direction of the shout. One of the flank riders had cut from the herd and was haring across the sandy sward towards him waving his Stetson.

He fought hard to focus his eyes on the image. 'Digger!' he responded, as the rider pulled rein up close in a cloud of dust. 'Goddamn! Well, I'll be . . .'

'I'd recognize the silhouette of that saddle slump from ten miles,' the man laughed.

Nahum wiped sweat from his eyes. He couldn't believe it.

'How you doing?' the man said by way of greeting.

'Getting by,' Nahum said, and waved an arm in the direction of the bawling cattle. 'How long you been with this outfit?'

'Couple of seasons now.' The man raised a hand to shield his eyes and looked about with a grin. 'And where are your cows?'

'Huh, ain't riding for the brand no more. Got laid off end of the season.'

'That's rough, pal. So what you doing out here on your ownsome?'

Nahum knew he could be open with an old workmate and, without going into exact whys and wherefores, told how it was important he locate a couple of riders last seen heading this way, and how the cattle drive had hampered his attempt to follow tracks.

When he described the pair, Digger nodded in recognition. 'You're in luck, pardner. Saw 'em a-whiles back.' He pointed. 'That a-ways. Must be the same ones. Woman – and the guy got one of them fancy black coats, just like you wus describing.'

'A Prince Albert.'

'Yeah. That's what I think they call 'em.'

'When and where?'

'Oh, about two hours back.' He aimed his finger again and added, 'They wus heading east towards the mountains yonder.'

'Digger, I been needing some luck and you've provided it, you son-of-a-gun.'

'Hey, you know me: happy to oblige, you old saddle-bum. Down to practicalities, how you doing for vittles?'

Nahum patted his saddle-bags. 'Ain't exactly starving yet, but could do with resupplying.'

'OK, get your hide over to the chuck wagon. It's way back with the drag riders. Like they all do, cook's complaining about being at the ass end of all the dust, but nothing you ain't heard before. Pay no heed to his groanifying. Just give my name and take what you want.'

After a shake of hands and a parting touch of his hat, Nahum gigged his horse.

*

Beneath him the big dun stallion came to a halt, switching his mane and tail at the droning flies. It was long since that he had picked up the tracks as described by his cowpunching pal but now the ground, hard earth and gravel, had become more difficult to read, the task made even tougher by the fading light. He eased his aching frame in the saddle as he took in the terrain. It was becoming rougher, rockier. For some time the ground had been rising and ahead the trail skirted an outcrop that marked the beginning of granite formation.

His fingers ran down the side of his head. The scrape was all but healed, itching a little in the sweaty heat, but the swelling was much reduced. Seeing no sign he reckoned his best bet was to maintain a straight line and hope. He'd have to bed down for the night soon anyhow.

He eased out the rein and tapped heels to send the animal forward. From then on it was nothing but the crunch of hoofs and the buzz of flies until, some half a mile on, the calm was broken by a jarring thunderclap. The spooked horse reared and Nahum fought with the reins and saddlehorn until he toppled from the seat. By the time he had righted himself, the animal was nowhere to be seen.

What the hell had happened? He looked across at the rock formation and, although he could see no activity, he assumed miners were blasting. After calling in vain for his horse, he laboriously scaled the nearest rock and raked the landscape. Seeing no sign of his mount, he reckoned there was nothing for it but to climb to a greater height for a better vantage point. The animal would have to be in one of the many rocky gullies.

'Ho, there, *señor*! Lost something?'

Nahum instinctively tugged the Remington free and turned to see a fellow emerging from one of the granite fissures. Fighting with the halter rope, the man was leading the cowman's shying, still frightened horse. The fellow was no more than medium tall, with a thin wiry build to him, rigged in the white cotton shirt and breeches of a Mexican peon, his face shadowed by a sombrero.

'He's OK, *señor*,' the man said, nodding back at the dun. 'And we don't mean you no harm. You can put your gun away.'

Noting a second figure appear behind him trailing two horses, Nahum kept a tight grip on his gun, frowning as he waited to see what tricks they might have for him.

Another Mexican, but unlike his friend this one was broad and thickset, his weathered features dark as mahogany, with thick black hair straggly under his sombrero and a beard that hid part of his face. A striped scrape covered his shoulders.

'That's right, *señor*,' the second man said. 'There is no need for the gun.'

Nahum lowered the Remington to a less threatening position while still keeping it available as the second man approached. Nahum was still taking stock of the two when yet another figure slid out from some bushes to his right, seeming to appear without a sound. Leggings of tanned hide, his feet shod with a pair of moccasins, his hat decorated with a clutch of white feathers spoke that he was more Indian than Mexican. A huge knife hung from his waist.

'We passed a mine back there,' the smaller man said.

'The miners, they told us to keep clear as they were getting ready to blast rock.'

'Ah,' Nahum said with a nod. 'I reckoned that was the cause.'

'Don't blame your hoss for bolting,' the man went on. 'Even though we were prepared for it, the blast nearly blew us out of our boots too.' He gave the horse a visual once-over. 'He don't look too much the worse for wear, *señor.*'

Nahum sheathed his gun and took the offered reins. 'Obliged.'

He patted the neck of the scared horse as the dun snorted and nuzzled his shoulder. 'Lucky we were coming by,' the sombrero'd man went on. 'An *hombre* cannot get far out here without a horse beneath him.'

'Names's Burnell,' Nahum said, remembering the name he had used when booking in the hotel back in Tyler. 'Jim Burnell. Glad to make your acquaintance.'

'I am Santos Ochoa and my *amigo*, we call him Valera. Happy to meet you, Señor Burnell.'

Nahum felt the strength in the man's grip.

'And this here is Aguila,' Ochoa said. He indicated the Indian who now stood silently, watching them both. 'It was him spotted you first. Way back when you wus jus' a little dot. Ain't much he misses.'

'Sure pleased to meet you,' Nahum said.

The Indian didn't answer, face remaining impassive.

The Mexican who called himself Ochoa looked more closely at Nahum's features. 'Seems to me like you might have hit trouble afore you come this far, if I ain't mistook.'

'Ain't on the run, if that's what you mean,' Nahum

grinned shakily, the touch of his hand grown wary as he felt at his still slightly swollen face. 'Found myself in a ruckus in a bar back in Allenville, is all.'

'I hear you, feller.' Ochoa's lean face didn't give away what he might be thinking. 'Figure that's your business, anyhow. Ain't that right, Valera?'

The addressed man nodded and asked, 'Where you headed, anyways?'

'North.'

'Hey, you're in luck,' Ochoa said, his voice easy and reassuring. 'We're heading north ourselves. It will be dark soon and we been keeping an eye open for somewheres to camp. How about you stay and eat with us tonight, an' we all head out together at first light? Nothing like company out in a nowhere place like this. How does that sound, *señor*? Cosy, eh?'

They had eaten a filling meal around the camp-fire. In the convivial atmosphere that wrapped around him right now, Nahum figured it was safe to ask the question. 'Business that brings me here, it has to do with two people, an' I reckon they have to be out here someplace.'

'Who would that be?'

'Feller an' a girl. I been following 'em out of Allenville.'

It seemed like something in the air changed right away, and suddenly the smiles were gone from all their faces.

'You have names for these folks, Jim?' Ochoa asked. The way Nahum heard it, his voice was a mite less friendly than before.

'Guess so,' Nahum nodded, scanning the sombre faces around him. 'Feller calls hisself Brad Carter, an' the lady answers to Rachel.'

'Is that right?' Ochoa breathed the words. His dark, black-stubbled features were set in a scowl. He'd have said more, but Valera laid a hand on his arm and the thickset man stayed quiet.

Time passed. Then Ochoa's dark eyes probed the cowman and he said, 'These two folk – they friends of yours, Jim? I mean, you knowing their names, and all.' Nahum met the other's gaze uncertainly, glanced to the silent figure of Valera and the Indian.

'Well now.' Nahum scratched the back of his neck as he thought over the situation not knowing quite how to play it. 'Not really friends,' he said slowly. 'Got a message for 'em, kind of, and need to catch up with 'em soon as I can.' He paused, eyes questioning the watchful faces round the fire. 'Ain't said nothing out of turn, have I?'

'Not a thing, Jim,' Ochoa forced an unconvincing smile. He hoisted his coffee mug. 'Drink up, feller. Guess we're just a little tired, is all.'

'If you say so,' Nahum shrugged and drank. All the same, when he spoke again he didn't sound too sure of things. 'You've run into them then, Carter and the girl?'

' 'Bout a couple of days back, I reckon,' Ochoa answered, sour-faced still behind the tin mug. 'Back at our place. We got a farm. Some miles north of Allenville. You coming up from that way and all, you might have seen it.'

Nahum shrugged inconclusively. 'Might have. Passed a few homesteads.'

102

'Put 'em up overnight at our place,' the fellow went on. 'Offered 'em hospitality as is our way. Fed 'em just like we done you here. Then they both headed north before first light. Ain't seen 'em since.'

He brought the cup to his mouth, eyes still hard on Nahum as he drank.

'Well, thanks, anyhow.' Nahum drank his coffee and set down the empty cup. To the cowman, it felt like the air had suddenly chilled around him, like there was something other than darkness taking away warmth. 'Guess I'm ready to bed down now, if it's all the same to you folks. It's been a hard ride all the way up from Allenville.'

'Sure, Jim.' Ochoa's voice was low and reassuring. His dark eyes, though, stayed watchful on the cowman as he withdrew a little from the fire.

'OK here?' Nahum said, pointing to where he was already sitting. 'I don't wanna hog the fire.'

'Of course, *señor*. Wherever. The land, she is free.'

Nahum took a blanket from his rig and settled down using his saddle as a pillow. After a while the rest of them finished drinking and bedded down similarly around the fire.

From time to time, he'd sensed a look sent his way, but when he glanced back it appeared they were sleeping soundly. Unease kept him awake for an hour or two, he guessed, but at last the weariness of the long ride took a hold, and he sank into the deeper darkness of sleep, his hand close to his gun handle.

A coyote barked somewhere out in the flat lands, and he roused suddenly, eyes opening on darkness as his hand went down for the gun in his belt. It wasn't there.

Nahum was still snatching around in the hope of finding it when he felt cold metal touch the side of his head, and he knew where his gun had gone.

TWELVE

'Just don't move a muscle,' Ochoa said to him. He held the .44 Remington close to the cowman's skull, his thumb resting easily on the hammer. 'One twitch from you, Señor Burnell, an' I might just pull this trigger. You better believe it, *amigo.*'

'What in hell. . . ?' Nahum stared at the lean, stubbled face that glared above him in the flamelit gloom. The flickering light played on the gun Valera also had trained upon him a little distance back.

Ochoa shook his head and laid a finger to his lips. He eased away from the man on the ground, still holding the gun level on Nahum's head. 'No call for you to say a word, *señor,*' the man told him. 'Now roll over, an' put both hands behind you.'

Nahum looked sideways into the muzzle of his own pistol, and figured he'd better do as he was told. He rolled on his belly, compliantly bringing both hands behind him. Above him he sensed fresh movement as Ochoa grabbed his wrists, looping them with what felt like rawhide thongs drawing them tight.

'Thought you had us fooled, did you not, *señor?*' the

big Mexican said. In the quiet of the night, his voice rang harsh. 'Just like them friends of yours. Well, maybe we got wise this time around!'

He made the knots fast and stood back, glaring at Nahum as the bound man struggled to turn his head. The two Mexicans seized his roped arms and hauled him into a sitting position. He made no effort to fight them, still wondering what was happening as a second rope went round his chest and shoulders. He sat where he was tied, grimacing as he fought the rawhide knots with the muscles of his wrists.

'You fellers mind tellin' me what goes on here?' Nahum asked. 'Just what in the hell did I do to you, that you got to hogtie me this way?'

'You got a poor line in friends, Jim,' Ochoa told him. The Mexican walked around him, the gun held firm in his hand as he answered. 'Carter and the girl stayed with us all right, just like we said. Come out of the flat land three days ago with some tale 'bout him was expectin' to come into some money an' just needed a little help.' He snorted, his lean face disgusted at the memory. 'Claimed the two of 'em had eloped, an' her old man was huntin' them – that Carter of yours can tell sob stories, right enough.'

'Looked like they'd been hauled through a cane-brake back of a hoss!' Valera muttered. 'And the way that gal looked was enough to break an *hombre*'s heart. They sure fooled us, an' that's a fact!'

'So we took 'em in, put 'em up overnight.' Ochoa's voice was bitter. 'Only thing was, next mornin' the both of 'em were gone. And so was the cash we had stashed in a mahogany box. Had over a hundred dollars in it, all our dinero from last season's marketing.'

The cowpuncher closed his eyes a moment. It figured. This Whelan guy seemed to have a penchant for grabbing anything he could get his hands on.

Ochoa nodded to his friend. 'Our intention is to get it back, but trouble is, me and Valera, we are mere workers of the land. We know nothing of reading sign. That is why we brung the redman. Back on the farm he helps us out when we need another pair of hands and he needs a dollar. See, he still remembers the old ways of his people – hunting and tracking. All that Indian kind of stuff. He's been cutting sign for us right up to here.'

He paused, eyes hard on the cowman. 'Yeah, these *bastardos*, they cleaned us out, Señor Carter and his whore. Some friends you got there!'

'Damn it, I don't know nothing about this!' Nahum struggled against ropes, anger and disbelief mingled in his voice. 'I ain't stolen from nobody in my life. An' I never said they was friends of mine, neither!'

'Maybe not.' Ochoa wasn't convinced, and it showed. The thickset Mexican pushed forward again, his stubbled face fierce and unforgiving as he leaned close to the man he'd just tied up tight as a heifer. 'But you sure hinted at it, *señor*. So, right now we ain't takin' no chances with you. Tell you somethin' else: we aim to catch up with these friends of yours an' git back our money. An' we don't want you on the loose while we're doing it – so you can come right along!' Anger thickened his voice, and he brought up his hand. Nahum had braced himself for the blow when he heard the Indian speak.

'There is not a need to hurt the man,' he said, his words coming slow and deep. It was the first time the

107

man had spoken. He stood a few yards further back into the darkness, and it wasn't easy to see him. Ochoa, though, caught the tone in his voice and breathed out fiercely, lowering his hand.

'Maybe you're tellin' it straight, *amigo*, an' maybe not.' Ochoa spoke more calmly, weariness showing in hard lines of his face. 'We had lost their tracks and Aguila had just cut sign of 'em again when you showed up.'

'They ain't my friends,' Nahum said, shaking his head. 'I came lookin' to find 'em. And the guy's name ain't Carter: it's Whelan, and he put me in a spot. The only way I can get myself out of the hole he put me in is to get my hands on him. That's why I'm out here. As to the woman he's toting around with him, they ain't eloping. He's just using her as a cover. And I need to catch up with them.'

'So do we, *señor*,' Ochoa said. The man weighed the pistol in his hand, considering the feel of the unfamiliar weapon in his palm. 'I know nothin' 'bout these things of which you speak. Like I say, you could be telling the truth, but Valera's right. We can't take no chances, not after what you told us about you being friends.'

'Yeah,' Nahum said, 'and I've told you that ain't true. I might have hinted at it when we first met up 'cos I didn't know which way the wind was blowing with you folks. So what happens now?'

'You stay put, an' don't cause no trouble,' the man said. He eyed the cowman and frowned, unsure in his mind.

'Got an idea,' Valera said, looking into the blackness ahead. 'We don't have to put ourselves to all this trouble, Santos. Especially with work building up back home all the time we're away.' He turned back to his companion. 'This *hombre*, he is a friend of the *bastardos*. His horse and rig should fetch something. Maybe even a hundred. If we help ourselves to them, we got our compensation – without riding the hell out of ourselves and our horses.'

'*Sí*,' Ochoa grunted. 'Why didn't I think of that? You got a brain under that sombrero of yours, Valera. Reckon we'll do just that.'

'And what about me?' Nahum wanted to know.

Ochoa, though, was no longer listening.

'You stay here, *señor*,' Valera said.

'Fixed like this?'

'Well, we're certainly not going to free you so you can come haring after us.'

'You don't give a guy much of a chance, do you?' Nahum grunted.

They ignored him, turned him over and one held him while the other cleaned out his pockets.

Ochoa did a quick count of the money. He handed some to the Indian. 'That pays you off for helping us.' He split the remainder and handed half to Valera. Then he unfastened Nahum's gunbelt, draped it over his saddle-horn and patted it. 'With all this and his horse, reckon we got our hundred,' he said. 'Now let's vamoose.'

'Come on, give me a break, fellers,' Nahum said.

They made no reply as the two mounted up and made off into the darkness with the Indian loping alongside them on foot.

Very quickly the sound of horses was no more.

In the silence Nahum fought vainly with the rawhide cords, flinching as the tight bonds cut into his flesh. Unlike the gun-toting gang back in the shack

Mexicans were men of the land and sure knew how to tie knots.

Some animal howled. A coyote? A wolf? Hopefully the fire would keep away any dangerous night creatures.

He wrestled some more with his bonds to no avail. He lay on his side looking at the glowing embers of the fire. There was no way he could use the fire to burn away the ropes without doing himself some real bad damage.

He writhed in an attempt to dislodge the bonds in hope it would give him a different purchase on them. But it was in vain. He rested and tried again. Didn't seem to be making any headway.

He didn't know how much time had passed when he thought he heard a sound. He paused in his efforts and listened. Yes, he could make out something. Something moving in the darkness. And coming nearer. Something weird, rhythmic. He listened hard, seeking the direction. What could it be? What could make such a regular padding sound?

Then a figure loomed out of the blackness: the Indian.

Nahum watched wide-eyed as the man drew the long-bladed knife from its sheath.

'What the Carter critter has done, I didn't know nothin' about,' Nahum said. 'An' they ain't my friends. It's the honest truth I told your buddies just now, even if they figure it was lies.' His eyes questioned the shadowy figure. 'You hear what I'm telling you, mister?'

'I hear you, *señor.*' The man didn't move from where he stood, the heavy knife now in the grip of both hands.

'They sent you back to kill me?' Nahum said. 'Is that

110

it? Paid you some more to get rid of the evidence?'

He breathed out, slumping back as his muscles eased their tenseness in the rawhide bonds. He stared at the stars. 'Just wanted you to know I'm telling it straight, is all.'

The man didn't answer, watching him gravely from the edge of the firelight. Seemed like it stayed that way for one heck of a while, the seconds going past like they were dragged on a leaden chain.

Suddenly the man took a pace towards him, brandishing the knife. 'No sound, *señor*.'

He pulled a rag from his pocket and pushed it into Nahum's mouth, holding it there as Nahum struggled and hauled on his ropes in momentary panic. The knife cut lower, shearing its way through the rope that bound. It cut again as the rope dropped loose, the rawhide thongs yielding as fibres gave to the keen-edged blade. Nahum sighed loudly in relief as circulation returned with a rush of pain to the veins in his wrists. The cloth in his mouth muffled the sound, and once he was quiet the Indian drew it away.

'It is in my mind that you talk straight, *señor*,' the man said. He sheathed the knife and stood back, watching as the cowman rocked and attempted to rub life into his arms.

The Indian moved away and for a while peered into the darkness, then nodded, turning back. 'You will follow the man and the woman, who went north from here?'

'I'm gonna try ... but with no horse, or tracks to follow ...'

'You'll not go back and cause trouble for Ochoa and his family?'

111

'No. Seems they're doing their best with a bad job and I got enough on my plate already.' Nahum's face showed grim in the dying firelight. 'Told you I come here to find the folk in the first place and I meant it. An' after what just happened, I figure I might have somethin' else to say to Whelan if ever I catch up with him!'

The Indian said nothing.

'Why did you come back?' Nahum said, as he concentrated on rubbing his wrists.

'Ochoa, Valera, they are good men at heart but sometimes they can be wrong. They are just simple workers of the soil with families to feed.'

'They called you Aguila?'

'That's right.'

'Spanish for eagle, ain't it?'

'*Sí.* I am of the Quechan tribe. My people are of the Yuman family. My tribal name, in your language, means Grey Eagle With The Sharp Eyes.'

Nahum worked his aching shoulders. 'How did your parents know you would have the skills of hunting to give you such a name?'

'It is our way to give a new name to a brave when he has grown to reveal the qualities that distinguish from others. Grey Eagle With The Sharp Eyes was given me in the second naming which comes when one of our kind matures. I was so dubbed according to the skills I had shown as a young brave during my time of testing. I favour the practice of name changing. Did not like the name of Little Mole.' He said something unintelligible in his own tongue. 'That is how we say my name but whites – whether Mex or Anglo – have trouble with our tongue so they call me Aguila.'

112

Nahum pulled himself to his feet and looked into the gloom. 'OK, Aguila. This Ochoa and Valera, how do you stand with them now you've let me free?'

'Huh, they do not know that I have freed you, *señor*.'

'What would happen if they found out?'

He shrugged.

'They close *amigos* of yours?' Nahum asked.

'Not close *amigos*. Like Ochoa said, they give me dollars from time to time when work gets too much for their hands alone on their plot. Huh, but they not my friends. They think I not understand the white man's money but I know they pay me cheap.'

'Listen, you doing me a favour makes us friends of a kind, I reckon. Would I be leaning too much on that friendship if I asked another favour? A big one?'

'What is your meaning?'

'I'm out in the middle of nowhere with no horse, nothing. I'm chasing a pair of bozos but I ain't seen tracks for quite a spell. The Mex said you can cut sign. So, would you help me track 'em? You know I got no money but I'll pay you when I can.' He paused and added, 'I know it's asking a lot but you did give me credit for being honest.'

The Quechan said nothing. He turned and dropped to the ground. 'We should sleep. There is still some time before the sun rises.'

The sun was just cutting across the landscape when Nahum woke. The fire had long died and the Quechan was watching him. 'I have found tracks. Come and when the opportunity arises I will catch game and we shall break our fast.'

113

He turned, beckoning Nahum to follow.

The cowman sleeved the sweat from his eyes, hauled himself to his feet and stumbled into the redman's tracks. A hundred yards on, he stole a parting glance at the place that had served as their camp before it faded back into the landscape, and the vast reach of the flat lands closed in on them both.

THIRTEEN

Nahum eyed the looming cacti as he attempted to keep up, glimpsed the shapes of bushes and assorted rock formations against the morning sky. It had been some time since they had eaten. Despite his tiredness, he forged ahead, eyes fixed on the constantly retreating figure in the vastness of the land that lay waiting for him.

Ahead, Aguila suddenly stopped in his tracks, his head moving one way then the other.

'What is it?' Nahum asked when he finally caught up.

'There is camp of redman close.'

Nahum scoured the environs. Could see nothing.

'The smell of roasting elk-meat is on the wind,' Aguila explained.

The white man looked quizzical. He couldn't smell anything.

'Come,' his companion said, and loped off at an angle from the course they had been following.

After a while, with Nahum still trailing behind, they approached a ridge. Through sweaty eyes the cowman saw a figure emerge over the distant top. By the time he got close he could see that the other man was Indian, he guessed a sentry, and the two men were exchanging words. Reaching the top Nahum looked down to see a small camp nestling beside a shallow creek.

Aguila beckoned for him to follow down the slope.

As they entered the camp they passed an old man working on bloody hides hanging from frames. Children played games on the hard ground, young squaws in leggings and buckskin dresses with fringes went about their business while old squaws were making balls of dough which they laid in the ashes of a fire.

Aguila had words with one of the braves and then was shown into a wickiup. A few minutes later he reappeared and gestured for Nahum to enter.

'I know these people,' the young Quechan said as Nahum joined him. 'It has occurred to me that it is bad thing for my friend to face his adversary without some weapon.'

Inside, an old man was unravelling a blanket which he had taken from a box, which revealed an old Dragoon pistol.

'Will this be of use?' Aguila asked. 'It was given to him in his younger days by a trader. He has no use for it now. Only problem, he says he doesn't know if it still works.'

'He got ammunition?'

After an exchange in native tongue, the old man extracted a pack of cartridges from the bottom of the box.

'When was the last time the gun was fired?' Nahum wanted know.

Aguila asked the question and translated the answer. 'Many, many summers. The redman rarely has need for sidearms.'

116

Nahum hefted it. 'And I reckon it was ancient when he acquired it,' he observed. 'You don't just fire an antique without some preparation. That's one of the easiest ways to get your hand blown off.'

'Are you interested?'

'Well, I do need a gun. Can they let me have some rags and grease?'

Outside, Nahum began to disassemble the weapon. As he cleaned and greased it, he acquired a wide-eyed audience of children. Then, he walked away from the dwellings followed by his curious retinue, held the gun at a distance aiming safely across the fields and pulled the trigger.

'Works OK,' he said after a couple of satisfying explosions. 'Just hope it's accurate.'

'It is etiquette to give the old man something in exchange.'

Nahum hunched his shoulders. 'I've been wiped out, what have I got?'

Aguila delved into his jacket and extracted a pocket watch on a chain. He wound it up and held it to his ear, then offered it to the old man who had come outside to observe the test. Delight showed in his eyes.

'First time we bivouac, I'll try the gun for accuracy,' Nahum said. 'Then I need to get in a bit of practice. Every gun's got its quirks and I reckon this baby will have its share.' He tried to stuff the thing into his belt. 'Trouble is, it's too big to carry like this. Pity a gunbelt doesn't go along with it.'

More words were exchanged and Nahum was eventually presented with a buckskin sack with a rawhide loop that he could put round his shoulder. He donned it and slipped in the gun. 'Hey,' he said, patting the thing in mock pride, 'what more could a guy want?'

Farewells were finally made and the two headed back up the slope.

'That was some timepiece you gave away back there,' Nahum said. 'I'm much obliged that you should be prepared to part with such an instrument.'

'It pleased the old man and I will not miss it. I have the sun for knowing the hour. The sun, it does not need a spring.'

'How much do you think it was worth?'

'Why?'

'I've got to put some figure on the bill. I promised I'd pay you back when I can and that means pay back for everything, watches and all.'

Aguila chuckled. 'Let's get back to those tracks of yours.'

The few folks who were going about their business showed little interest in the lone rider making his way along their main street. Likewise, Eugene Whelan showed little interest in them. In fact, the only interest he had in their poky little jerkwater town was as a possible source of funds. And that possibility seemed remote now he had noted that the sole bank in the place was closed.

He needed to top up his travelling money. He was getting through the stuff like a prairie fire.

There were a few stores, none looked a roaring success and he reckoned their tills were likely only to contain cents, maybe a few bills at most. Didn't look the kind of town where such establishments did any worthwhile business anyway. Last place at the end of town was the funeral parlour and he would have passed that too and rejoined his woman out of town, had he not stopped at the trough to water his horse. While he was doing so his eye caught a quality-dressed dude approaching the parlour and pausing at the door. What specifically caught Whelan's attention was the fellow pulling out a bulky wallet and checking its contents against a piece of paper. The man extracted some bills and entered the establishment.

The guy had all the look of a customer coming in to pay off an account. A big fat customer with a big fat wallet.

Whelan glanced along the street, saw no one in proximity and casually crossed the street, looping his horse's rein loosely over the tie-rail. He stepped quickly up onto the boardwalk. A glance through the black-draped window was enough for him to learn there were only two in the place.

Gun in hand he slipped through the door.

It was hours later that Nahum and his Indian friend trudged down the same street. They availed themselves of water at a trough and plumped themselves wearily on the boardwalk edge.

After a while an old guy came ambling along the walk-way and dropped into a cane chair behind them. 'You got a smoke for an old veteran, stranger?'

Nahum threw a glance back. 'Sure, grandpa,' he said, and passed over Mike's makings, one of the few things the Mexicans had not taken.

The man slowly put a cigarette together. 'You just come to town?' he asked as he returned the bits and pieces.

119

'Yeah.'

The fellow lit the cigarette and watched the rising smoke for a moment. 'You missed all the excitement.'

Nahum wasn't interested – he'd got a few other things on his mind – but out of politeness he said, 'Oh, yeah, what was that?'

'Feller robbed the funeral parlour. Bold as brass, just walked in and whacked the undertaker and the mayor. Took over a hundred bucks from 'em. Huh, mayor sure chose a bum time to drop by to pay off his sister's funeral.'

Now Nahum was interested. 'Who was this feller?'

'Nobody knows. Some stranger who'd just moseyed into town all casual like. Yeah, rode in real slow but I tell you what – he rode out a sight faster!'

Nahum raised his eyebrows, looked at Aguila, then back at the man. 'What did this feller look like?'

'Don't seem to be much available by way of details – he was in and out before anyone noticed him – 'cepting the two guys he buffaloed say he was dressed more like a funeral director himself. Big black coat and stuff.'

Nahum pushed the makings back into his pocket. Then, 'What happened?'

'Well, 'cos it was the mayor he robbed and put on the floor, all hell broke loose. Marshal got a posse together and lit out after the critter.'

'The story of my life,' Nahum said casually. 'Wherever I go I always miss the fun.'

Feigning lack of interest, he yawned and said nothing for a few moments before asking casually, 'Which way this guy go?'

The man pointed down the drag. 'Western trail.'

Still registering indifference, Nahum rose. 'See yuh, pal.'

'Got all the sound of Whelan,' he said when they were out of earshot of the old fellow.

'And what is my friend's plan now?' Aguila wanted to know. 'To wait and see what happens? If these men catch him and bring him back your problem is solved.'

'No it ain't. For my problem to be solved it is necessary that *I* catch the jasper with my own two hands. You been a great help to me, Aguila. I owe it to you to give you the whole story.'

He told about his part in the prison breakout and subsequent events.

'I do not understand the workings of the white man's government that you describe,' the Quechan said when Nahum had given the fuller account, 'but I see why it could be to your benefit for you to be the one who should catch this man called Whelan. Unfortunately, it appears it is now out of your hands. There does not seem much you can do, my friend.'

Nahum reflected. Then, 'Maybe so, maybe not. Come on.'

They walked over to the saloon. Noting the *No Indians* sign outside, Nahum gestured to his companion to stay and pushed through the doors alone.

'Sorry, but ain't got the money for a drink,' he said at the bar. 'But I'd be obliged if you could point to where a stranger could get a look at a map.'

The barman eyed the dust-covered, unkempt visitor. 'You got the look of a pair of guys who I hear tell just *walked* into town.'

'Yeah, that's me.'

121

'Our little settlement being miles from anyplace, ain't many travellers *walk* into town.' He poured a couple of whiskies and pushed them across. 'On the house. One there for your Injun pal, too.' He scanned his existing customers. 'Nearest map would be at the Land Registry Office, wouldn't it, fellers?'

'Yeah,' came the response.

Nahum gave his thanks and rejoined his companion. After he had returned the empty glasses the pair made their way to the Land Office. The clerk there was obliging.

'I'm a stranger in town,' Nahum said as he peered at the map on the wall. 'Where exactly are we?'

'Not only a stranger but you sound lost, pardner,' the clerk said. 'Well, we call this place Encounter. It's only in small letters but you'll find it there someplace.'

Nahum studied the map more closely, his finger picking out the names of Tyler, Allenville and Encounter in turn. He looked knowingly at Aguila, then traced out a line between them and beyond. 'You could run a straight-edge against them,' he whispered.

He followed the line on, his finger resting on letters spelling Celebration.

'Find what you wanted?' the clerk asked.

'Maybe. Thanks, pal.'

'Did my friend learn anything?' Aguila asked when they were outside once more.

'Think so. Tyler, Allenville and Encounter – as near as damn-it they're following a north-east tack. I'm guessing that bearing ain't a coincidence. If I'm right, the place he's heading for is Celebration. It may not be his ultimate destination – following that line would take him right into Colorado – but I'd put my last dollar on Celebration being his intended next port of call. That's if he can get clear of the party presently hot on his tail.'

'But he was seen heading west.'

'From what I know of Whelan I reckon that when he rode in he was looking for some easy cash and wasn't expecting to have a posse after him. I'm guessing on the spur of the moment he chose to head out that way in the hope of putting them off. Come on. According to the map back in that Land Office there's a trail that curves to the north-east – the trail to Celebration.'

An hour out of Encounter, Aguila dropped to a crouch by the side of the trail, his fingers exploring the grass and sand. 'Horse joined the trail here from the west not too long back.'

Nahum looked at the slight indentations in grass and sand which had caught the eagle eye of his companion. 'I'm hazarding that was Whelan. From what we hear he had a start on the posse. There's a big chance he used his time advantage to circle north around the town and rejoin his woman on this trail.'

But it was a long shot and Nahum knew it. Not only was he grabbing at straws but he'd long been aware that his quarry had the advantage of being on horseback. The only element in the mix that gave him a modicum of satisfaction was the notion that a woman from an Eastern city was not likely to be an experienced rider and could slow him down a little. One hope, but a thin one.

Whelan was single-minded. With $50,000 at stake, most guys would be. On that assumption, Nahum speculated that when Whelan reckoned he didn't need the woman as a cover anymore – maybe when he got close to his hidden cache – he would drop her like a branding iron left too long in the fire.

And the more he thought about these things as the two ate more trail dust, the more he felt his luck was running out. There are only so many straws a man can grab at. He was in this low state of mind when Lady Luck teased him with a little break. The two tired men were overtaken by a wagon. There was an elderly couple aboard who were headed for their homestead a short stretch this side of Celebration. Hitching a ride on the slow moving vehicle was not exactly winning the jackpot but it upped the trackers' pace a little, as well as providing some rest for their weary legs.

FOURTEEN

Stephen Cassidy Esquire leant back from the table and watched the waiter pour his coffee. Editor of the *Celebration Chronicle*, he always treated himself to a restaurant meal after he had put the weekly paper to bed. And, as was his way, the latest copy of the paper bore the 'Esquire' title against his name, a reminder of the habits of an East Coast upbringing.

Right now, his assistant Luke would be covered in ink, working at the presses. Or so he thought.

He paid the check, adding his usual tip to the saucer, and lit a cigarette. The sound of distant hoots prompted him to take out his pocket watch. He flicked open the lid and checked the time. 'Yuma train dead on time,' he said to himself. 'As usual.'

He had returned the watch to its pocket and taken another sip of coffee when he was surprised to see an ink-smudged face at the window. Under the ink and through the murk of the glass, his assistant Luke was recognizable. And the man was waving frantically.

Cassidy gave his employee a look that reflected a mixture of puzzlement and irritation, then signalled through the window for the fellow to go round to the front of the restaurant.

Outside he was met by his employee with one of the town's old-timers alongside.

'What is it, Luke?' the editor said irritably.

'A story's just come in, sir. I've taken the decision to halt printing in case you want to include something about it in the Stop Press. I know how you like the paper to be up-to-date, sir.'

'And what's this story that is so important that printing should be stopped?'

'Some gunplay, sir. Right here in town.'

'Gunplay? I've heard no gunfire.'

'Well, not gunplay in the sense of shooting, sir, but a gun was drawn and used to put a man into custody.' He gestured to the fellow at his side. 'Old Tom here saw it. Came over to the newspaper office to tell us.'

'OK, Tom, give me details. Where did it happen?'

'Outside the hotel, sir. Fellow came out. Seems like he'd got a horse ready to leave town. But looked like this other fellow was waiting for him. Pulled his gun, disarmed the fellow and marched him off. Bold as brass.'

'This guy with the gun, was he law?'

'Didn't see no badge, sir. And seems he had a redman with him.'

'Where did they go?'

'Went down the drag. Last time I saw 'em they were going past the hardware store.'

Cassidy nodded. 'Could be heading for the railroad station,' he concluded. 'Thanks, Tom.' He turned to his employee. 'Luke, you were right to put a hold on the printing. A guy pulling a gun on Main Street is first-page material. We might have to do some major resetting. Get back to the office and wait for me. Keep your hold on printing while I see if I can fill out the story with some details.'

He stepped into the middle of the street and looked the length of the main drag. Couldn't see the men. He crossed to the boardwalk and made his way along to the hotel where a horse stood at the tie-rail. He entered to see a well-dressed young girl, seated on a couch in the foyer, sniffing into a handkerchief.

Walking over to the desk he was greeted by the clerk. 'Hear tell of a bit of business outside a short while back,' the editor began. 'Something about some feller being taken into custody. Can you give me any details for the next edition?'

'Didn't see much, Mr Cassidy,' the clerk said. 'Just caught a glimpse through the window beforehand of the guys who were waiting. Paid 'em no never-mind at the time. Only knew what happened when the guy's lady over there came back in after the ruckus. That's his horse still out there.'

The newspaperman threw a glance at the girl, then looked back at the clerk. 'This fellow, he registered at the hotel?'

'Yes, sir.'

'Name?'

The register was turned so the editor could see the entry. 'Hm,' he said, noting the name. 'Brad Carter, eh? Thanks.'

He touched his forehead in acknowledgement, crossed the foyer and sat beside the girl. 'Local paper, miss. I was wondering what you can tell me about events.'

She didn't seem to hear him. 'Just left me, he did. No reason. Just said I'd outlived my usefulness. What does that mean? Sold my horse too. Now I got nothing but a piece of change he stuck in my hand.'

'What was your relationship to him, miss?'

No response.

'Why was he being taken away? Who took him away?'

Again she didn't seem to hear. She simply stuck out her hand, exposing a couple of crumpled bills. 'Said that was to be going on with. What did he mean by that? And how far is this going to get me? After all I've given up for him too!'

'OK. Where was Mr Carter going on the horse before he was waylaid? You know, the horse tied up outside.'

She suddenly brightened. 'The horse! Yes, the horse!'

Seeing he was getting nowhere, Cassidy rose. 'I'd like to speak to you later, miss. Will you be here so that I can ask you a few questions?'

'The hell I will! I should get a good price for his horse and its equipment!' Her voice and body displayed she had acquired a new energy from somewhere. 'Hey, I heard a train whistle a while ago. That means I can get a train back East! Should be able to get enough cash to buy a ticket and get the hell out of this God-forsaken place!'

Editor and clerk exchanged looks of mutual incomprehension, as the newspaperman moved towards the door. Outside he progressed once more along the street.

At the railroad station he presented himself at the ticket window.

'Howdy, Mr Cassidy. What can I do for you?'

'Working on something for the paper, Buck. Last train out to Yuma, did a couple of guys get on?'

'A whole passel of folks boarded, Mr Cassidy. Anybody in particular?'

'These two would be together. Maybe an Indian with them.'

'Oh yeah.' The station manager chuckled. 'Now you mention it, you couldn't get a couple of guys more together. One had his wrists roped and the other was stuck to him real close. Guess he was some kind of lawman. Pulled his gun when his prisoner got awkward about boarding.'

'This lawman, he got a badge?'

'Didn't see one. Just assumed he was law. Hey, you think he was one of them bounty hunters I heard tell of? Never seed one before. You think he was?'

'I know less than you, Buck.' Cassidy pulled out the notebook he always carried. 'As I said I'm looking for something for the paper. Can you give me anything else about them? Physical descriptions, for example.'

'The one with the gun was a tall guy in range clothes and the other looked a bit of a dude. You know, long black coat an' all.'

'Anything else?'

'No. Apart from some Injun hovering in the background. Can't tell you much about him 'ceptin' he just looked like an Injun.'

'Thanks.'

The editor turned to leave when the stationman said, 'Oh, there was one other thing: I think I caught one of their names. Seems like the lawman, if that's what he was, addressed his prisoner as Whelan. Something like that.'

The newspaperman stopped in his tracks, turned and came back. 'Whelan? Are you sure?'

'Like I said, can't be sure. But it sounded like it.'

'Thanks.'

Cassidy returned to his office where his assistant was sitting beside a motionless press. 'Luke, it appears there was nothing much in the tale after all. Just carry on, run the paper as it stands.'

'Anything you say, boss.'

Cassidy stepped outside and looked along the street.

The tentacles of the telegraph system were increasingly spreading around the country, reaching even remote parts of the West such as a little-known train halt with the name of Celebration. And by such means Stephen Cassidy Esquire had received a communication a few days back from a long-unseen relative, his cousin Frank Lyle. Errant in his ways, Frank was still a relative and there were obligations. Stressing it was of the utmost importance, the cable had asked for any information the newsman could get on some fellow by the name of Whelan.

He headed for the telegraph office and sent a message.

FIFTEEN

The train bound for Yuma had been rolling for a long time. They were on the last lap. Not much could happen now. With the bag containing the Dragoon resting on his lap, Nahum looked away from the window and closed his eyes for a moment, still sensuously contemplating the luxury of padding against his weary frame.

A rummage through Whelan's pockets had revealed more than enough money to cover their fares and now his prisoner was opposite, head nodding, apparently asleep. But Nahum was taking no chances. Not till this baby was back in the slammer. And he opened his eyes again, glancing at Aguila who was on the far side of the car looking out of the window.

Nahum stretched and looked back. Among the scatteration of passengers in the car were a husband and wife with a couple of noisy children. Further back a handful of occupants whiled away their time: some kind of businessman; an old lady dozing with her head against the padding; a lone cowboy absent-mindedly watching the passing scenery, his gear stacked nearby. On boarding Nahum had taken stock of them all then paid them no mind.

He leant towards the Indian. 'Keep your eye on him. I'm gonna find out if there's a privy on this bone-shaker.'

He made his way along the swaying aisle to the end, eventually locating the lavatory stall. When he'd used it he was making his way back when, towards the end of the car, he noted a seat stacked with saddle, saddle-bags and saddle-holster. Adjacent a fellow in range gear was stretched out, his feet resting on the opposite seat his spurs just clear of the padding.

'Another cowman without a mount, if I'm not mistaken,' Nahum said in a jocular tone as the man looked up.

'Yeah. You too?'

'Me too.' Nahum indicated the saddle boot on the seat. 'Good looking gun you got there.'

The man leant over, pulled the weapon from the scabbard and offered it for inspection. 'Yeah, Winchester. The thing was my pa's. Saw him through his working life and now it's serving me just as well. It's getting on but wouldn't part with it for a heap of dollars.'

Nahum hefted it, sighted it and passed it back. 'A reliable old stalwart.'

The man patted it affectionately and returned it to the scabbard. 'Yeah.' Then, 'So you're a 'puncher too, eh? Who with?'

'I rode for the Big K a-whiles back. Only they ain't so big no more, laid me off.'

The man grunted. 'Same story here. Started my working life in Texas but had to move out this way and now the Mid-West beef business has taken a plunge. Railheads running down, couple of winters from hell. I heard the Kansas beef trade is thriving but I'm heading out to

California. My brother's got a job lined up for me with an outfit out there. And you?'

'Couldn't get fixed up with a cattle outfit again but managed to get set on by a freighting company. Ain't as bracing as a life on the open range – and it's taking time to get used to boneheaded mules, I can tell you – but it kills time and money's good.'

'A wagonner, eh? So what are you doing out this way without your wagon?'

'Got myself into a bit of a tangle.'

'Oh yeah?'

Nahum saw no need for taking it any further. 'But looks as though I'm getting through it. Then it's back south to flicking traces over the backs of mules, I guess.'

'Well, good luck, pardner.'

Nahum reciprocated the well-wishing with 'Same to you, Tex', returned to his seat and responded once more to the padding.

Noting Whelan was still asleep, he looked out of the window. It was that way for a long time. Then, through a sudden shower of glowing embers from the stack, he noticed the track begin to curve, enough for him to see a water tower in the distance. A likely stopover. The land was as desolate as the terrain they had been crossing for the last few days. Save for the water tower, nothing out there big enough for a horned toad to bother hunkering under.

Then he started. As the angle of their approach changed he could make out some horses by the tower. And four men in long grey slickers. He got Aguila's attention and pointed. The Indian made to speak but Nahum nodded at Whelan and touched his lips for silence. As the train began to slow, he was certain he had seen the men before, back in the shack up in the hills: the bank-robbers, with an axe to grind.

That was enough for him. But how had they known he would be on this train?

'Keep your weather eye on Whelan here. There's guys that spell trouble at the halt. Looks like things might get tricky.'

'I am with you, Nahum. How you figure on tackling it?'

By now the big stacker was moving very slowly. 'For starters, I'm taking our friend Whelan for a walk.'

'What for?'

'Ain't figured exactly. Matter of looking for opportunity. But ain't nothing for slowing down a game like the pot disappearing. Meantimes, you make yourself scarce.' He didn't want to involve his generous friend in a squabble that wasn't his. 'And keep a weather-eye open. Take care, my friend.'

The Quechan made off down the aisle and Nahum's gaze returned to Whelan. The man's back was to the halt and he still had his eyes closed, so was unaware of impending developments. 'Come on,' Nahum said, grabbing his neck and shoulder. 'Move your ass.'

'Hey, what the hell's going on?' Whelan spluttered.

'You an' me's stretching our legs, pilgrim.' He forced his captive into the aisle before the man had a chance to look out of the window. At the end he stopped by the man with the saddle equipment. 'Looks like there might be some trouble, Tex,' he whispered. 'That tangle I mentioned. If anything happens, try to get all the passengers out of the way, especially the kids. And do a fellow cowpoke a favour: lever a load into that Winchester and lay it on the floor under your seat out of sight.'

The man glanced through the window. 'Those guys out there?'

'Yeah.'

The man crossed the aisle and yanked at the handle of the Winchester. 'Done.'

Keeping a tight grip on Whelan's back so that the man didn't move too far forward and be seen, Nahum pushed him towards the window. 'Try not to be spotted and look to your right. Don't know if you recognize those particular bozos, but they're your pals. The ones you robbed a bank with. The ones who got you sprung from Yuma.' He yanked the man back. 'You know what that means? They're after you. If they get their hands on you and extract their information from you, your life won't be worth a plugged nickel. Now, I've got my own reasons for them not to get their hands on you, so your only hope is me. Remember that and do everything I say without a quibble.'

As the slowing train drew level with the waiting horsemen, Nahum chanced another look. Revealing as little as possible of himself he took stock of the faces as the human tableau rolled by. All were dusted and unshaven; all were studying the train, probing the windows for faces. He recognized all of them, especially two. The hefty square-faced bruiser he'd heard described as Hagan, the one who liked punching folk when they were tied up, the one he reckoned killed Mike. And the small, emaciated rheum-eyed leader.

Nahum had seen enough, but what to do with his prisoner? Where could he hide him? Then an idea started forming. But was it possible?

He moved back a little. 'I want to borrow your ropes too, Tex,' he said, nodding to the cowman's gear.

The ropes in his hand, he moved towards the door and checked. Now they were well past the waiting quartet he pushed Whelan onto the platform.

'If you know what's good for you, you'll keep quiet and simply do as you're told. Like now, I'm saying jump.'

With that he pushed the man so that the two of them dropped, fetching up in the sand on the off-side before the train stopped. Nahum looked about him, his brain working overtime.

It was several minutes later. Alone, Nahum was walking alongside the now stationary train. He could hear voices and clatter inside the cars and he figured the gang had boarded and were searching the thing.

He glanced back to see that the fireman had shut off the leather water hose and was unhooking it to swing it back toward the tower. Nahum was just about to haul himself up into a car when a man dropped from the platform of the last car. It was the hefty one known as Hagan. He had a mean look and an even meaner-looking gun on his hip as the grey trail coat billowed out with his movement. 'He's here!' he shouted.

Nahum thought quickly and leapt up, into and through the car. He dropped down to the sandy ground on the other side, ran partway along the length of a car and rolled onto the track. From that position he could see Hagan's boots thumping alongside the train.

When the big man's feet disappeared Nahum rolled clear and bounded to his feet. As quick as he could he loped across the space and stepped behind the fence beside the water tower. He waited until he confirmed that he had been seen by one of the men, then emerged doing up his trousers in an exaggerated fashion suggesting that emptying his bladder had been his reason for leaving the train.

He sprinted back and entered a car. Through a window he saw Hagan lumbering towards the fence. The man took a look behind it and, seeing nothing but a fast-drying urine stain, did a quick circuit of the tower. Seeing nothing amiss he headed back to the train.

Nahum dropped onto a seat, keeping his eyes skinned but within seconds wood splintered near his head. He dropped down and grappled with the hide bag to extract the Dragoon. He had not anticipated any gunplay. The gang didn't want him, they wanted Whelan. And they would know that their objective would be thwarted should they kill him.

'Better give up, cowboy,' someone boomed. 'You don't stand a chance. And you know what we want.'

Nahum peered below the legs of the benches and could see boots advancing. Glass shattered above him as another bullet came his way crashing through the window. 'Play it your way,' he said, lining up and triggering the old weapon. There was a scream and a grey-slickered figure collapsed in the aisle. Nahum came out and looked down at the robber moaning over the wound just above his ankle. He picked up the man's gun and threw it through the broken window. 'Your own fault, pal. Just 'cos you didn't see a gunbelt didn't mean I wasn't toting a gun.'

Suddenly the far door broke open and revealed the

137

old lady he had seen before. Obviously the Texan hadn't managed to get all the passengers out of the way. She was gripped by one of the gang; looked like he might have a gun at her back.

'Throw down that gun or you'll be responsible for this dear old lady getting something nasty. You wouldn't want that on your brush-popping conscience would you?'

Nahum slung the Dragoon on a seat.

'That's better,' the chief said, pushed the woman aside and began to move down the aisle.

Nahum walked backwards as the other advanced. The robber picked up the Dragoon and looked down at his groaning friend. 'Bit of a mess you made there. But at least you didn't kill him, I'll give you that. Hagan reckoned you'd have some kind of weapon in that bag. But you got nothing now, have you?'

Nahum wrenched at the knob behind him and darted through the doorway slamming the door behind him. He leapt over to the next car only to find himself running into Hagan's levelled gun.

'Led us a merry dance, ain't yuh, Crabtree?' the gang boss said, as he followed through and entered the car. 'Well, sonny boy, the music's stopped. Where's Whelan?'

'Who?' Nahum said in mock innocence. He saw no harm in dragging out the verbal cat-and-mouse. Soon wheels would be turning once again and each revolution would mean that Yuma was all that much nearer.

'You know who,' the boss continued. 'Eugene Whelan. Our Eugene Whelan. Don't play smart-asses. We got the firepower. We know you got on the train with him back at Celebration.'

138

He went to the door. 'Wessels, come here! We got the cowpoke!'

He returned and motioned to Hagan. 'Did you see any sign of Whelan out there?'

'Nothing, boss.'

'Sure? You looked all over?'

'All over, boss. He ain't there. Gotta be on the damn train somewheres.'

'What you done with him?' the chief asked again of Nahum jabbing his pistol into his stomach.

Suddenly the train lurched forward, wheels frictionizing on rails. The crew of the locomotive were aware of the trouble and must have figured the sooner they got to the station and civilization the better.

At that moment Wessels, the remaining gang-member, appeared and looked around the car. 'You got Whelan then?'

'Not yet,' the boss hissed. 'But this hobo's gonna tell us where he is, ain't you?'

'Shall I get this thing stopped, boss?' Wessels suggested, as the car juddered. 'He might have hidden him back at that halt. He spent some time there.'

'No, Hagan's checked it over. Crabtree ain't stashed him near the water tower. Land's all open there, nowhere to hide anything so Whelan's on board somewheres.'

'But what about the horses, boss?' Wessels asked. 'We can't leave 'em.'

'Screw the horses. There's more at stake than a few horses. Just hold the feller tight so we can persuade him to be co-operative.'

Nahum felt himself gripped by strong arms.

139

The chief put his face up close. 'So where is the thieving bastard?'

No response. The leader nodded to Hagan who slammed his ham fist against Nahum's chin.

'We got our sources,' the chief said. 'So we know all about you boarding with him back at Celebration.'

Nahum rocked with the motion of the train. His arms still pinned, he wiped his bleeding mouth against his shoulder. He glowered at Hagan. 'You like doing that, don't you, you big ox?'

The boss raised a hand to stop another mallet hand doing its work. 'Now, brushpopper, for the last time, what you done with our mutual friend?'

Nahum shrugged. 'His passage is booked to Yuma. And there ain't nothing you can do about it.' This time it was the boss's pistol butt that came down, its sharp end biting into Nahum's neck. 'Don't give me that bilge. We're still in the back of beyond. You couldn't have arranged nothin'. He's on this rustbucket somewheres. Wessels, have a look over it again. Every nook and cranny.'

The tall man heavy-footed aft.

The wheels clicking over end-rails ticked away the minutes. Wessels returned down the aisle. He shook his head as he passed them, disappearing forward. Ten minutes later he returned, a perplexed look on his face. There was dirt on his hands. It was clear he had been as far as the engine and still come up with a no-play-hand.

The boss flicked his eyes at Hagan who got the message and slammed a hard fist into Nahum's stomach.

'Where is he?'

'Matter of applying logic, ain't it?' Nahum wheezed

140

when he'd got some of his breath back. 'How much of that commodity you got?'

'What's that fancy talk mean?' the crook wanted to know.

'Think about it. We stopped, didn't we? Back at the water tower. And you say you know he was in my custody before then – and he ain't no more. So . . .'

'You didn't leave him there. You couldn't have. Hagan gave it the once-over. You looked everywhere, didn't yuh?'

The big man nodded. 'Yes, boss.'

'There was one place he didn't look,' Nahum said.

'What you mean?'

'In the water tank itself.'

The chief looked at his underling. 'Did you look in the tank?'

'No, boss.'

'Was there any way of gettin' up to it?'

'Come to think of, boss, there was a ladder.'

Silence. Then the boss snapped, 'Ass-hole!'

He glowered at Nahum for a moment, and then the tension eased from his features. 'You couldn't have put him up there. You didn't have time to get Whelan up no ladder – not that high. You're just trying to play for time, ain't yuh?'

'That's something for you to puzzle on.'

Suddenly the train hit some uneven track and everybody staggered. Nahum took advantage of the short interruption to wrench himself loose. He shot forward, executing a forward roll down the aisle and flipping behind a seat. A gun exploded and a chunk of upholstery disappeared from the top of the furniture.

'No use hiding, cowboy,' Lyle shouted. 'You can't do much to stop us. You ain't even armed!'

Nahum groped under the seat to locate the Winchester the cattleman had hidden. He rolled back into the aisle firing from the floor. Wessels fell back, a bloody patch in his shoulder.

Nahum suddenly heard whimpering and saw he was alongside a woman cringing beneath the seat as bullets whipped the length of the car. Damn. One of his reasons for heading into this car was that he'd thought it empty.

Both the boss's and Hagan's guns barked. Nahum rolled across the aisle to limit danger to the woman.

He made it just in time. Varnished wood splintered, glass shattered and lead was thick in the air. His thoughts were still on the woman and the possibility she could be in the crossfire. 'Keep your head down, ma'am,' he said and sent some lead of his own along the car.

Then he noticed the only gunfire was his own. He paused and listened; quiet except for the whimpering of the wounded Wessels. More, he was aware that the noise of wheels on track had become louder. He guessed what that meant. He took a fleeting look along the aisle. Yes, the door at the end had been opened. He sprinted up the walkway, stopping only to pick up the loads left for him by the Texan. Fetching up against the seats close to the end of the car, he jacked in loads.

The end door was flapping open.

'They sure mean business,' the woman said.

'So do I, ma'am. That's why there's only two of 'em left.' He thought and listened. 'They've backed off for a reason. But still keep low, ma'am. Reckon one of 'em

142

might try his hand at getting at me through the windows.'

He eyed the glass. 'If he's capable one of 'em could hang down from the roof and get a bead from a window.' He looked at the line of windows. 'Trouble is, I don't know which one he'd be firing through.'

'What you gonna do?'

His eyes showed he had an idea. 'Only thing for it. Beat 'em up to the roof. Remember, keep your head down, ma'am.'

With that he bounded down the car and leapt up onto the seats, legs straddling the aisle. He slammed at the small lock of the skylight window with the butt of the Winchester. As the lock screws gave, the frame swung down and he was hauling himself up.

The smoke from the bell stacker was thick in his lungs but he didn't mind; the important thing was he had the roof to himself. The car swayed and lying prone not only reduced the chance of being jolted off but lessened the target he presented.

He gripped the catwalk and, matching the rhythm of the car, began to ease himself forward. At the end of the car he looked over the edge. Nobody. He got slowly to his feet, then leapt to the next car.

He gradually worked his way further forward but suddenly the rhythm of the train changed as it hit a downgrade. He slumped forward and just managed to grip the catwalk. He adapted himself to the new rhythms of the train beneath him. But too late.

There was a shot behind him. The wind whipped away the sound but he saw the wooden roof score inches away from his hand. Maintaining a one-handed grip on the catwalk he turned.

Hagan was on the top of the car behind him! Grinning, enjoying his advantage. How the big man had got up so fast and how he was now maintaining his position Nahum couldn't figure; but he was erect, legs apart, gun poised for another shot!

Nahum wasn't in circumstances to fire fast and accurate. But he didn't have to. Inexplicably the man bent backwards. Nahum took his chance and fired. The man spun with the impact of the bullet, groping at his side. As he bounced off the roof like a kewpie doll, Nahum caught sight of a knife in his back.

He peered back over the side, just in time to see the man hit the cinder fill, face down. Under the momentum the man flipped over revealing his features. The visage was a crimson pulp; and Nahum could just make out the receding whiteness of teeth showing through lacerated lips. The over-sized Hagan was not going to kill any more little old men tied to chairs.

Then Nahum noted the Quechan waving a hand, just visible over the edge of the roof at the other end of the car and he knew where the knife had come from.

He waved in return and inched along the roof in the opposite direction. At the edge he chanced a look below. Both platforms on either side of the coupling were deserted. He dropped down. He felt more secure with something flatter under his feet. But he didn't notice his shadow fall on the glass of the door.

The frosted window shattered and he collapsed, gripping the rail. He'd felt a searing line along his arm. Against a succession of shots, he looked down the sleeve of his shirt. There was blood. His arm was scored, but nothing vital.

He pulled himself up, wincing at the use of his arm. He hopped across between the cars and smashed open the door with his boot.

The car's few passengers were standing back apprehensively. There was a groaning gang-member on the floor. But, more important, the white-coated chief was at the far end, fighting with the lock on the door.

'End of the line, Lyle!' Nahum shouted, 'There's only you left.' The gang leader turned as the cowpuncher continued, 'I need a clear run to Yuma so you're disembarking here and now. And I'm taking Whelan in.'

'What do you mean?' The man's gun was still in his hand, but not levelled.

'First you drop the gun,' Nahum ordered.

The man thought about, then did so. 'You got me cold-decked. Maybe we can talk this thing over, Crabtree. There's a lot of money at stake.'

'We'll talk it over – outside,' Nahum drawled, moving slowly forward. 'Back off. Through the door.'

The man complied.

'The money,' the boss said when they were on the windswept platform, 'it's all we want. You can have a cut. Like a reward.'

'I'm only interested in taking Whelan in. Sorry about shooting your men, but my liberty, not to mention reputation, are at stake here.' He pointed to the edge of the platform. 'Now jump. With a bit of luck you'll get away with a bruising and maybe a sprained ankle. No more than you and your boys have been dishing out to me. You'll survive.'

The man saw the determination in the cowman's eyes, and looked fearfully at the passing ground. Then,

145

resolved to the action, he said, 'OK. But just tell me one thing. Allow me one question: what you did with Whelan?'

'Like I said. He's already on his way to Yuma. In fact, the way things are, he'll reach it way ahead of either of us.'

Before the little man could ask another question Nahum had shoved him and he'd disappeared. The cowman went to the edge and looked back. That the man was writhing by the side of the track meant he still had some life in him. Yes, he'd survive.

Suddenly the old woman was behind him along with a wide-eyed conductor. 'Is it all over?'

'Yes, ma'am.'

'Well, let me see to your wound,' she said, noting the blood dripping from inside his sleeve.

'Much obliged, ma'am, but in a minute.' He looked at the conductor. 'Can you stop the train for a couple of minutes?'

'Why?'

'Got myself some freight that needs relocating.'

'There's a limit to messing around with the operation of Southern Pacific rolling stock, mister, and you've exceeded it already. I allowed you on this train with a prisoner because you said you were on official business. You couldn't show me a badge because you said you'd lost everything. Mighty strange, but I accepted your story. Now there's been bullets flying all over the place. This vehicle is not stopping.'

'A man's life could be at stake. Stop the train or on your head be it.'

'What do you mean?'

'Give the signal.'

'I should do as he says.' The voice had a Texan drawl. Nahum didn't need to turn to know who it was. 'Listen, pal,' the man continued, 'this guy's a regular guy and has been up against some tough opposition. For that he's got my respect and he should have yours.'

'All right but it'd better be important,' the railroad man said. 'I assure you, mister, when we get to Yuma you're gonna have to account to Southern Pacific for all these untoward events.'

'When we get to Yuma,' Nahum grunted, 'I got a lotta accounting to do.'

As the wheels grated to a standstill Nahum and the Texan dropped from the steps of the car. Seemingly out of nowhere Aguila suddenly appeared and was silently padding beside him. Nahum slapped him round the shoulders in thanks. 'Don't forget to put that knife on the bill.'

Still puzzled, the couple followed Nahum to the front of the huge locomotive.

'Well, I'll be!' the Texan exclaimed, joining him at the business end of the bell stacker. Neatly bound across the top of the cowcatcher was Eugene Whelan, shaken and aching but none the worse for his uncomfortable ride.

'It was the talk of the train,' the Texan said, eyes still wide, 'a-guessing what you'd done with him!'

'Now *that* is against regulations as well,' the conductor said, mustering up his best officious tone. 'Him being up front – like this.'

'Well look at it this way,' Nahum said as he started to pick at one of the knots. 'You could say it's just another instance of Southern Pacific aiming to satisfy its customers.'

147

'What do you mean?'

'Well, this feller's the kinda passenger who likes to know where he's going.'

SIXTEEN

Two bedraggled men moved towards the Sallyport. One was roped. Behind him the other had a bandaged arm and wielded an old Dragoon pistol.

A guard toting a shotgun stepped forward. 'State your business.'

'Just come in on the Southern Pacific,' Nahum said, nodding back to his prisoner. 'Got something the warden will be interested in.'

The uniformed man looked the two over, giving Whelan especial attention. 'The warden expecting him?'

'Doubt it. So it'll probably be quite a surprise. But I'm sure a pleasant surprise.'

The sentry nodded to one of his colleagues. Keys clanked and the gate swung open.

Some twenty minutes later, Whelan was in a cell and Nahum was in an office standing opposite the warden who was seated at his desk.

'I recognize the prisoner but I don't recognize you,' the official was saying. 'I don't see a badge. Which agency are you with?'

Nahum indicated the bloodstained bandage. 'Mind if I sit, sir?'

'Go ahead.'

'The thing's complicated, sir. You'll remember a wagon came delivering lumber to the penitentiary and Whelan was aboard when it left. Ever since, you been after Whelan and the couple of guys who were driving that wagon. Well, I'm here because I was one of those guys. The other, an old guy, has since died so he's out of the accounting.'

Then he filled in the details of the story.

'I invited you to my office in order to thank you for bringing Whelan in,' the warden said at the end of the account, 'and now you tell to me you were one of the instruments of his escape! That puts a different complexion on things.'

He shook his head. 'Must admit, can't see why you've declared yourself as one of those who sprung him. Don't understand why you didn't keep your head down. You're taking a hell of a chance coming here.'

'I know, and that's the point. I didn't say I sprung him. I said I was on the wagon that took him out of here. I didn't know what the deal was about until we were well clear of the prison.'

'You trying to tell me you were an innocent party in the break out?'

'Yeah, and that's why I brung him in. To get the record straight.'

'I appreciate your honesty, mister, but that issue ain't in my hands. It'll be up to some judge. Now you've presented yourself we're gonna have to follow the book on this. And I'm gonna have to ask you for your gun.'

The bailiff's voice boomed out around the courtroom, 'The defendant will rise to hear judgment.'

Since Nahum had been imprisoned Pat had visited him regularly. When he had told her the story and they had talked through his defence, he had asked if Aguila could work for the company in payment for his help and she had been only pleased to oblige. And the selfsame redman was now sitting alongside his new employer in the first row of the public benches.

Nahum had never had any dealings with the law before and had found himself in a complicated whirlwind of legalities. First, there had been a preliminary hearing to see if there was a case to answer. He needed legal representation but with his having little funds the court had appointed an attorney.

The fellow was an otherwise unemployed drunk and had bungled his way through the proceedings so badly that the judge had no recourse but conclude there was a case to answer. Nahum had been retained in custody pending the proper trail.

Now, a week later, he was standing once again before the court. He knew this was the big stuff when an out-of-town judge wearing a black robe had swept in and mounted the bench.

The new circumstances were intimidating all right but all was not lost. During the intervening week, word had got around Rios that Nahum was an employee of the local and much respected freighting company. More important, it had become known that he was especially close to Pat Slaughter, whom townsfolk had watched grow up and for whom they had a great fondness. As a consequence, friends had started a fund, got townsfolk to chip in, resulting in enough to finance a competent lawyer.

It was now noon, the trial having been in session for most of the morning.

Nahum threw a brief glance behind him in Pat's direction and rose to hear judgment as he had just been instructed.

He didn't understand the legal mumbo-jumbo that constituted the judge's preamble but he understood the conclusion.

'It is the opinion of this court that the accused was a blameless party in the matter of the escape of Eugene Whelan from Yuma Penal Institution. We see no reason not to take his word when he says that he believed the exercise to consist of nothing more than the simple delivery of a consignment of timber to the prison. There is nothing in the record to show that we should think otherwise. Of course, that he didn't question some of the strange aspects of the exercise suggests that he may have been naïve but naïvety is not a crime. Likewise, we see no reason to question his veracity when he says that when he discovered the true nature of the situation it was too late and he was not in a position to do anything about it. That is, not immediately following the escape.'

The judge's voice rose. 'Moreover, that this is the true account of his part is supported by his subsequent actions in returning the said Whelan to his rightful place behind bars. Therefore we find the defendant innocent of all charges. The week that he has already spent in custody awaiting legal proceedings is deemed as sufficient punishment for any minor transgressions. Case dismissed.'

Pat ran round the rail and threw her arms around him. 'Oh, darling, I knew they'd see sense.'

'I was hoping so but, must say, you had more confidence than me.' Over his shoulder he winked at the beaming Quechan who had risen but was keeping a diplomatic distance from the embracing couple.

'Come on,' Pat said. 'Let's get out of here.'

On its feet the audience clapped the couple as they walked between the benches and out into the daylight.

'You know,' Nahum said, as the two embraced under the warm Arizona sun. 'I been questioned a lot this last week. Now I've got a question for you. Will you marry me?'

EPILOGUE

Under the hot Colorado sun a bunch of men in long grey slickers were peering into a hole. A couple of them had been digging long enough to work up an extra sweat. Now, some twelve inches down they could make out the shape of bags under the dust.

'This must be it,' the leader said.

And so it was confirmed when they had extracted the bags from the top of the coffin in the grave.

'What is going on here?'

The gang turned to see a priest scurrying across the graveyard. 'Mother Mary!' the pastor exclaimed, crossing himself dramatically when he saw the opened grave. 'Desecrating one who is at peace with our Lord. This is sacrilege!'

'Calm down, Father,' the little man with the foxy features said, 'we ain't touched the coffin. There was something of ours on top of it is all. And we're gonna put the earth back like nothing has happened.' He pushed some coins into the priest's hand. 'Put that in the poor box, or buy yourself some communion wine. Now make yourself scarce.'

'But, but . . .'

The leader grunted in exasperation and pulled back his coat displaying a heavy pistol. 'Get your holy ass out of here, Father.'

When the pastor was too far away to observe details, the bags were dusted off and the money counted.

'Not quite fifty grand, boss,' the counter said. 'But close.'

'That figures,' the boss said. 'Whelan would have taken a handful to be going on with. Now fill the grave back in. Real neat and tidy.' He made the sign of the cross across the front of his slicker. 'Remember, we're on hallowed ground.'

He watched the men until they had completed their task and then he looked down the hill towards the town. 'I do believe I saw a saloon when we rode in. This calls for a celebration. After the time we spent expending sweat on this matter I reckon we deserve it.'

An apprehensive priest peering round the side of the church door watched his unwelcome visitors as they left the cemetery, mounted up and headed down to the town.

They were walking along the main drag towards a saloon when the boss spied a bank. He stopped and smiled. 'Let's give someone a surprise. We couldn't have located the money if that Crabtree guy hadn't chased Whelan and got the spalpeen's ass hauled back inside. We owe him something for that.'

He turned to one of the men. 'Wessels, take a couple of grand and get yourself over to that bank. Have them make out a bank draft to that amount and send it to Crabtree, care of Slaughter and Tough, Rios. Frank Lyle always pays his debts.'

When Wessels was on his way the rest continued to the saloon.

'Whiskey,' the little man said as he stumped up to the bar. 'How much for a bottle?'

The barman told him and Lyle pushed coins across. The three sat at a table and the boss filled their glasses.

'To a mission accomplished,' he said, and they clinked their raised glasses in the middle of the table.

Smokes were lit, glasses replenished and the men settled into some relaxed talk.

The youngest man in the group, a recent recruit to replace Hagan, was looking puzzled. 'Say, boss, I still don't know how the stolen money was located out here in this God-forsaken place in the wilds of Colorado.'

'When Whelan was back inside, I figured we couldn't try to get him out again. The authorities would be wise to another attempt at springing him but we still needed to know where the cache was. Hell, Whelan could have stashed it anywhere between Kansas and Arizona where he ended up. So I pulled strings and got a fellow con to put the notion to Whelan that if he didn't divulge the where-at of the cache he wouldn't be breathing God's good air for much longer.'

'From what I've heard Whelan is a tough boyo,' the youngster said. 'He can handle himself. Surely a threat like that wouldn't make him spill?'

'He's a tough one, all right. But it was pointed out to him that if he didn't comply he'd have to keep his eye permanently on his back. He'd never know which cons were in my pay. That's the way I work. Best thing for Whelan was to cut his losses and cough up the information – which he did. As it turned out he gave a good description of this place in Colorado – the town, the cemetery, the name on the grave. And here we are.'

At that moment Wessels returned from the bank.

'Help yourself,' Lyle said, pointing to the bottle and a glass.

'Good sentiment, boss,' Wessels said, after he'd downed the drink, 'giving Crabtree a handout like that. Wraps up everything neat, kinda poetic. We got the money back, or at least most of it, Whelan's back where he belongs and young Crabtree gets some recompense.'

'Heard tell young Crabtree got married,' Lyle said.

'Yeah.'

The chief smiled. 'Hey, be something to see the look on his face when he gets that bank draft as a belated wedding present. He might be feeling a little fretted about us, but he should figure who sent the money and that should be enough to tell him we don't hold nothing against him for winging a couple of our men.'

'But he did more than that, boss,' Crocker put in. 'Ain't you forgetting he put paid to Hagan?'

'Hell, I don't count that against the brush-popper. Hagan had always been a liability. I was glad to see the back of him. But I have to give the young cowpoke his due, he was only trying to sort out his own problems. Can't hold that against a feller. And he sure had guts and perseverance. I admire that in a man.'

'I see what you mean, boss. Everything wrapped up neat.'

Then the charitable look disappeared from the chief's face. 'But that's not quite the end. All Whelan's done by spilling the beans about the location of the money has

157

been to earn himself a little time. And I mean a little. He'll not see the outside of Yuma again. Tomorrow, next week, next year, sometime he's gonna meet with a nasty accident. He crossed me – and nobody gets away with crossing Frank Lyle.'

He rose. 'Drink up, men,' he said. 'And cork the bottle. It'll serve as refreshment on the journey back. We got a long way to go.'

The four stepped out into the sunlight.

'OK, let's hit the trail,' Lyle said, moving towards his horse.

'You ain't going nowhere,' a voice boomed. The hands of the four went for their guns as their eyes raked their surroundings.

'And if you use those you'll be blasted to hell.'

Three men with levelled rifles and packing stars partially disclosed themselves from cover, two at their sides and the speaker across the street.

'Do as you're told,' said someone behind them. Lyle glanced back to see another two similarly armed coming through the saloon door. 'Drop your guns.'

'He's right, men,' Lyle breathed. 'We don't stand a chance.'

'We been trailing you for a coon's age,' the man in front of them said, as he stepped across the street. 'So long in fact I feel like I know you, Frank. We just been holding back in the hope that you'd lead us to the loot.' He nodded at the saddle-bags. 'Which you've helpfully done.'

Minutes later the four were being handcuffed.

Lyle smiled wryly in resignation as he pondered on his shackled wrists. 'Say, Mr Lawman. Any chance of us serving our time in Yuma?'

'What's got into you, Lyle?' the man with the badge said. 'You've been in the game long enough to know that with the bank robbery being in Kansas, that's where you're going and that's where you'll serve your time – once we've got clearance for extradition from the authorities here in Colorado which is just a routine matter.'

The gang-boss scowled and the officer looked quizzical. 'Anyways, why would you be interested in doing your spell in a hell-hole like Yuma?'

'Oh, just some unfinished business,' Lyle grunted.

Not understanding, the lawman shrugged and indicated for his prisoner to mount up. When he had settled into the saddle Lyle muttered something under his breath.

Virtually unintelligible but it sounded something like, 'Nothing that can't wait.'

And the wry smile returned to his sharp-featured face.